HELEN SEEMED TO SHIVER AS IF IN ANTICIPATION OF SOME SECRET AND FORBIDDEN PLEASURE. THEN SHE ROSE AND EXECUTED A DELICIOUS CURTSEY TO THE THREE MEN.

'Doctor, we are at your service. Let us go to the dinner as if we were the priests and priestesses of the Goat Song of ancient Greece and enjoy our meal as if it were the eating of a God. The curtain is up, the play begins. Soon the streets of London will witness the lust of our hunt. Soon a human being will tremble. Soon the jaws of our trap will yawn greedily for their victim. Soon our altar will once more be bathed in human blood.'

'These are noble sentiments, Madam, and I savour your expression of them,' said Lipsius gravely. 'Allow me to escort you into dinner.'

THE
DEVIL'S
MAZE

by Gerald Suster

PENGUIN BOOKS

To Ann
and in memory of Arthur Machen

ROC

Published by the Penguin Group
Penguin Books Ltd, 27 Wrights Lane, London W8 5TZ, England
Penguin Books USA Inc., 375 Hudson Street, New York, New York 10014, USA
Penguin Books Australia Ltd, Ringwood, Victoria, Australia
Penguin Books Canada Ltd, 10 Alcorn Avenue, Toronto, Ontario, Canada M4V 3B2
Penguin Books (NZ) Ltd, 182–190 Wairau Road, Auckland 10, New Zealand

Penguin Books Ltd, Registered Offices: Harmondsworth, Middlesex, England

First published in the USA by Dell Publishing Co., Inc. 1983
Published in Roc 1994
10 9 8 7 6 5 4 3 2 1

RoC Roc is a trademark of Penguin Books Ltd

Printed in England by Clays Ltd, St Ives plc

Contents

Prologue

1—The Adventure of the Crowded Restaurant   19

2—The Encounter of the Hansom Cabs   35
     The Man in the Stove-pipe Hat

3—The Incident of the Gentleman Attacked
     by Footpads   65
     Many Spaces and a Time

4—The Unfortunate Young Lady of the Savoy   91
     The Spaces In Between

5—The Amusements of the Demented Doctor   117
     The Other One Just a Doll

6—The Adventure of the Recognised Conspirator   161
     Soul Mates

7—The Connoisseur of the Curious and Unusual   187
     The Devil's Maze

8—The Enchantress of St John's Wood   215
     The Image That Counts

9—Strange Occurrence in Kensington   233
     The History of the Young Lady with
     Flaming Red Hair

10—The Adventure of the Respectable Residences   247

     Epilogue—By the Author   253

And they stripped him, and they scourged him, and they sent him unto a certain secret place which was known unto the Alchymists of old time, wherein he wandered a thousand Years, but never chanced upon That which he sought, since he only discovered Doorways into Nothingness and divers curious and many coloured Windows, on account of which that Place is called The Devil's Maze . . .

JASPER HERRICK (1634–1690)
The Hermetic Quest Of The Splendours of Saitan

Amid the smog and respectability that are in the popular imagination thought to represent the fabric of the Eighteen Nineties, there nevertheless flourished beneath this crust poisonous growths and monstrous orchids, beings that took the outward semblance of humankind, murder, magic, rites older even than civilisation, devils, fiends, labyrinths of the damned . . .

KONRAD F. DIETRICH (1879–1975)
The Undercurrents Of History in Western Culture

Prologue

It was dusk in the Autumn of 1897. Above the grey housetops, the sky glowed with a dull red, while a fresh wind whipped the dusty dead leaves along the pavements of Sheen Street, which is in the comfortable and elegant area of Marylebone. Outside one of these quiet and respectable residences, a hansom cab had halted, and an individual in a high bowler hat and baggy morning-coat was engaged in the process of paying the cabman, who seemed more than satisfied by the sum of two shillings and sixpence. As the cabman drove off, the man in the bowler hat strode swiftly to the maroon front door, seized the chunky brass knocker, and rapped loudly three times.

The man's appearance was hardly ingratiating. His complexion, the colour of molten wax, was not noticeably improved by a thick ginger moustache which melted into a pair of bulbous chin-whiskers. His eyes were small and a muddy brown, his teeth large, uneven and discoloured, and his cheeks looked heavy and swollen. He did not look correctly dressed for either the hour, or the area,

11

but the butler who had opened the door admitted him immediately, and showed him into a large drawing room in a manner that betokened respect.

The room was simply but expensively furnished. There were large oak presses, two bookcases of extreme elegance, and in one corner a carved chest which must have been medieval. A man and a young woman, both dressed at the height of fashion, occupied a sofa in the far corner.

'Good evening, Richmond,' said the man, who was smooth and clean-shaven, and who would have struck an observer as being either very languid, or very bored. 'I trust that your unfinished business has now been completed to your satisfaction.'

Richmond returned something that could have been a smile, but was more a vile leer.

' "In business, the first requisite is despatch", ' he quoted, somewhat pompously. 'I agree with Mr Addison, and I have despatched him. Before I did so, he told me everything we wanted to know. You always enjoy spinning things out, Davies. I don't believe in prolonging the agony. I finished him quickly.'

'How intensely dull,' murmured Davies, and added: 'What about the body?'

'Disposed of in the usual way.'

'It would be too much to hope for a souvenir, I suppose,' said the girl, lacing her tone with more than a tinge of sarcasm. Her figure was striking,

she had a quaint and piquant rather than a beautiful
face, and her eyes were of shining hazel.

'Stop it, Helen,' said Richmond testily. 'You
know I cannot abide that barbarian custom of yours.'

The girl laughed.

'How very civilised of you, Richmond. You are
so much a product of this dismal age in which we
have the misfortune to live. No exhibit for the
doctor's museum? Why, I do believe you have
missed your vocation. You should have been a
sober and practical man of business, something in
the City. I can just see you persuing your *Times*
over your morning brew of tea and muttering outraged platitudes about Oscar Wilde and ''the unclean cult of the sunflower''.'

'Sometimes I feel I shall never understand you,
Helen,' Richmond retorted bitterly. 'I killed him,
and we have all the information we need. Isn't that
enough?'

'No,' said Helen. 'It is not enough. You are
not an artist, Richmond, you are but a common
labourer, and murder without artistry possesses all
the excitement of boiled cod. If Davies is the
Aubrey Beardsley of crime, then you are merely
murder's William Powell Frith.'

'I think that's quite enough squabbling for the
time being,' Davies cut in as Richmond endeavoured to control his twitching facial muscles.
'Squabbling is so unartistic. I see no harm in us
approaching crime in our own ways so long as

those ways are not bourgeois. Our friend Richmond may approach murder in the manner of a shilling shocker while you prefer the admirable refinement of Monsieur Huysmans, but there is surely nothing wrong with the shilling shockers which all decent-minded persons desire to ban. I confess I read them myself, and derive great profit and enjoyment. Let us not forget the triumphs which the three of us have achieved. Who could forget the drama of Doctor Melmoth's madness? Or the Order of the Red Hand? Or the search for the jewel of the Inmost Light? Or even the quest for the Young Man with Spectacles?'

'But you never did find the Gold Tiberius, did you?' interrupted a soft voice from the direction of the door.

The three friends looked instantly at the man who had just crept silently into the room. He was a portly middle-aged individual who, to all outward appearances, radiated benevolence and serenity from his bald crown to his short, plump legs. Two features, however, detracted from this pleasing impression. One was the tight, compressed mouth, the lips of which were moist. The other was the eyes, small, yellow, beady, and hooded by fleshly eyelids.

'Good evening, doctor,' came three respectful voices.

'Good evening,' the man returned evenly. 'You may relax. I do not wish to discuss past mistakes.

Pray be seated, Richmond. We have more pressing matters upon our hands. Some sherry?' The butler entered and proceeded to serve them.

'More pressing matters?' echoed Davies. 'Do you by any chance refer to the Blood Quest, Dr. Lipsius?'

'Indeed, my dear Davies, indeed. I await the tale of Richmond's adventures of today with the utmost expectation. Proceed, my dear Richmond. I anticipate that you will not disappoint us.'

Dr Lipsius seated himself and proceeded to enjoy his glass of amontillado; Richmond cleared his throat and began to talk, while Davies and Helen listened attentively. The monologue lasted one hour, during which the glasses of all four were frequently replenished. At last Richmond ceased, and there was silence for a few moments.

'Good,' said Dr Lipsius. 'Splendid. It is better than I thought. I cannot resist the conviction that our efforts will be crowned with success. We cannot afford failure.'

'On a Blood Quest, doctor, we have never failed before,' put in Davies.

'Then obviously you will not fail this time,' returned Lipsius. 'You know that I employ you only when a matter demands subtlety, ruthlessness and artistry. You will require more of these qualities than ever before, for the hunt is not without danger. I want living human blood, my friends, and I mean to have it.'

'Doctor, your aim is wholly enchanting,' said Helen, 'and I assure you that you will find our performance to your liking.'

'How very glad I am to hear you say that, Helen,' said Lipsius silkily. 'I look forward in greedy anticipation to witnessing your exquisite cruelties when the dance of the hunt is behind us.'

'It will be a pleasure, doctor.' The girl smirked, and tossed back curls of rich black hair. 'But listen to our director.'

'Well, Davies?' Lipsius enquired.

Davies lit a Turkish cigarette and inhaled deeply.

'You spoke just now of ''the dance of the hunt'', my dear doctor,' he said at last. 'Very well, we shall have a ballet. We shall perform a ballet of the kind that we have had once before when we hunted the Young Man with Spectacles. Once more shall we take to the streets of London and become what we are not. Once more shall commonplace alleyways and busy thoroughfares be the stage for a drama of the damned. So important is our victim that our performances will have to be the finest of our respective careers. I do not think that we will disappoint you, doctor.' He smiled.

'Davies is right,' chimed in Helen, her hazel eyes shining. 'The finest plays should always be performed before the unseeing eyes of the dead whom we call the citizens of London. I have played many parts in my short life, and I long now to act once more.'

'Yes, I believe I would also like to have another crack at acting,' Richmond agreed. 'What do you think, doctor?'

'I was delighted by your exquisite performances of three years ago,' pronounced Lipsius, 'and I bitterly regret that I was unable to witness the climax. Flawed though the structure of the drama was, the production and performances were quite impeccable. I would welcome a triumphant return.'

'I knew you would be pleased,' cooed Helen, whose thighs were tightly crossed beneath her black silk dress and voluminous petticoats. 'I pray that the script we shall enact will prove enchanting, and that we are given parts which prove as exquisite as they may be taxing.'

'Oh, the plot is charming, my dear,' murmured Davies, 'though more I think for us than for our intended victim.'

'Admirable,' said Lipsius, 'wholly admirable. But I see that we have consumed more than our customary quantity of amontillado, and I do believe that dinner awaits us. After we have enjoyed our repast, Davies will relate the plot of the Blood Quest which he envisages, and then,' the thin lips momentarily parted in a smile, 'it will be time to partake of the Rites of Avallaunius.'

Helen seemed to shiver as if in anticipation of some secret and forbidden pleasure. Then she rose and executed a delicious curtsey to the three men.

'Doctor, we are at your service. Let us go to

dinner as if we were the priests and priestess of the Goat Song of ancient Greece and enjoy our meal as if it were the eating of a God. The curtain is up, the play begins. Soon the streets of London will witness the lust of our hunt. Soon a human being will tremble. Soon the jaws of our trap wil yawn greedily for their victim. Soon our altar will once more be bathed in human blood.'

'These are noble sentiments, Madam, and I savour your expression of them,' said Lipsius gravely. 'Allow me to escort you into dinner.'

'With my glad consent, Dr Lipsius,' Helen answered as she took his arm. 'Yet even now a fire rages within me which I fear that your burgundy cannot quench.'

'I do not mean to quench it, Helen,' Lipsius responded, 'but to inflame it. Come. It is always best to feast before a kill.'

I

The Adventure of the Crowded Restaurant

Mr Charles Renshawe was a gentleman of refined tastes and eccentric habits. The friends he possessed regarded him as being a little more than slightly mad, but were more than willing to endure this characteristic for the sake of his wines and his conversation. His generosity with the former somehow lent the strangeness of the latter a greater degree of acceptability. For although Renshawe was barely thirty, his love of travel and a hunger for all manner of experiences had given him a most unfashionable lack of inhibition.

It was true that there were those who shunned him and who repeated and enlarged upon the rumours that had surrounded him ever since he had come down from Oxford. It was said that his private life was scandalous, that he indulged in the study of ancient rites and mysteries, that he performed rituals more suited to pagan groves than Christian churches, and that while engaged upon his travels, he had fraternised with native women in a manner that suggested a singular lack of propriety. Renshawe never bothered to deny these tales for the simple reason that they were, for the most part, quite true.

He was a tall lean man, with dark straight hair, and a moustache and beard that gave him a slightly Mephistophelean appearance. His eyes, which were usually a very clear blue, now possessed a slightly glazed appearance, which was probably due to the small pipe of opium which he had just completed smoking. It was nine in the evening, and as he poured himself a small glass of cognac, he reflected upon the design of the living room in his recently acquired flat, and decided that he approved of its blend of austerity and unashamed luxury.

The carpet that covered it from wall to wall was Persian, and was fashioned in the form of a mandala. The curtains were of dark green velvet. Upon the wood-panelled walls hung an original Beardsley, a Whistler etching, and a landscape by an obscure artist called Cézanne, which he had purchased for a few pounds in Paris some years before. The furniture consisted of a sofa, two comfortable armchairs, a plain mahogany sideboard upon which reposed a case of duelling pistols, a solid writing-desk of the same wood, and a high teak bookcase. A glance at the contents of the latter assured the casual peruser of its owner's interests.

There were morocco-bound volumes of Huysmans, Poe, Baudelaire, Verlaine, Rimbaud, Swinburne, and Dowson in addition to the works of an

author whom all respectable persons had banished
from their bookshelves since his imprisonment,
Oscar Wilde. There was *The Yellow Book*, *The
Savoy*, Gautier's *Mademoiselle de Maupin* and
Moore's *Confessions of a Young Man*. Upon the
top shelf resposed many bizarre and arcane works
like Levi's *The Ritual and Dogma of High Magic*,
Barret's *The Magus*, the works of Agrippa and
Paracelsus, and *The Book of the Sacred Magic of
Abra-Melin the Mage*.

Renshawe had just raised his glass to his lips
when there was a knock upon the door. He rose,
walked through the hall to the door, and opened it
to reveal the sight of a strikingly beautiful young
woman.

'Clarissa!' he exclaimed, bowing to kiss her
small gloved hand. 'How exquisitely delightful it
is to behold your charms once more!'

'It is entirely my pleasure, Charles, to be the
acknowledged cause of your deliciously romantic
delight,' replied the lady, entering the living room
and looking around her. 'It has been far too long,
but unquestionably worth enduring, if this is the
new Renshawe residence. It has my unqualified
approval.'

'And your delectable attire has mine,' said
Renshawe as he took her cloak and gazed admir-
ingly at the green silk evening gown which graced
her nubile body. 'Do take a seat. What can I offer
you? I have wine, if that is what you would prefer.

Alternatively, I have just smoked a small quantity of excellent opium, which I heartily recommend. Or something equally exotic?'

'I think almost anything, even Fourpenny Ale, would be a relief after the tedium which I have had to endure this week,' replied Clarissa. 'You know, Charles, it can be so awful being Lady Mountford and having to behave sensibly. I admit that at times I enjoy it enormously, but this last week has been like a play by Mr Henry Arthur Jones. There never seemed to be an end.' She laughed softly, showing dainty white teeth. 'Do you have any hashish by any chance? I think that and a glass of port would suit my requirements admirably.'

'You are in luck, Clarissa. My apothecary in Mayfair keeps me supplied only with the finest; I think you will enjoy my latest purchase. It is altogether so pleasurable that I remain convinced that it is only a matter of time before the Reverend Mrs Grundy and her band of ever hopeful kill-joys discover its existence and prohibit it by Act of Parliament.'

Clarissa laughed again and removed her hat, allowing her blonde curls full freedom. Her blue eyes stared impudently at Renshawe.

'Come, Charles, stop battling the dragon of prudery,' she teased. 'I would hate having to visit you in Reading Gaol. Just serve the refreshments and let us enjoy them without moralising. Some-

times you are quite as bad in your own way as that
insufferable novelist Mrs Humphrey Ward.'

They had known each other for two years. He
was the son of a prosperous man of business who
had left him a few thousand pounds a year, while
Clarissa was the only offspring of an American steel
magnate, and had married into the English aristo-
cracy. 'Our marriage,' she had told Renshawe,
'was one of those commercial transactions of which
our age is so fond. I acquired a title and a country
seat, and my dear husband received the where-
withal to pay off his gambling debts. Poor fellow,
he was wholly impotent, which rather suited me as
he was exceedingly ugly. I fear I was not unduly
distressed when he died in the cholera epidemic.'
That had been three years ago, since which time
Clarissa had acquired the reputation of being one
of the most attractive and extraordinary women in
London. Her dinners and receptions were legendary,
and although her unconventionality made her un-
popular with some, she took care never to do
anything overt enough to invite public censure.

It was true that at her dinners impoverished
poets and artists sat with the wealthy and powerful
and were treated with equal courtesy, and this had
offended some, who were in consequence never
again invited. She had scandalised others by
subsidising soup kitchens in the East End in which
one did not have to sing hymns or say prayers for
one's supper. Others whispered about her private

life, but in the main, her immediate social circle was too rich to care provided she was discreet, which she usually was.

The one thing which her acquaintances found impossible to understand was Clarissa's interest in the occult, which she never bothered to explain to them. They would not have understood that for her, socialising was but an amusing game, and money existed only to be spent. Nor could they have comprehended her desire to experience the intensity communicated to her by poets and artists, a desire which had led her upon a quest for a wisdom beyond the material. At last she had found a society dedicated to the extension of consciousness and the search for the Light, and that was where she had met Charles Renshawe.

Since that time, her life had changed, but inwardly rather than to outward appearances. She enjoyed letting people think of her as merely an intelligent and fascinating flirt, but beneath that mask she pursued her studies and practices with seriousness and dedication. She did not entirely understand what motivated Charles Renshawe, nor could she grasp in what strange realms of the imagination his mind moved, but she did realise that within the body for which she hungered there lay a wisdom that might slake her thirst for the mystical and marvellous.

Renshawe handed her a small pipe and a glass of vintage port, then sank into his armchair and lit an Egyptian cigarette. For a few minutes they smoked contentedly in silence, then Clarissa said:

'Charles you are being so uncommonly quiet that you must be bursting to tell me something.' Renshawe arched his eyebrows. 'Now you are endeavouring to look nonchalant. I remain unconvinced. Tell me of the progress of your hunt for Dr Lipsius.'

Renshawe smiled and sipped a little brandy.

'You know me too well,' he said at last. 'I realise that I have not told you very much beyond the fact that Lipsius is perhaps the most poisonous individual in London. Yet he is more than that, Clarissa. Our Order, as you know, is pledged to a quest for the Light. Dr Lipsius heads another Order which is dedicated to the Prince of Darkness, an Order which seeks to plunge the world into an eternal night in which the only sounds are of weeping and wailing and of gnashing of teeth, and which engages in ceremonies and abominations which would turn the stomach of the most hardened reprobate. Lipsius has but one goal, and that goal is power, and his slimy tentacles reach into the realms of politics, business and crime, corrupting all whom they touch.'

'Is it known what this man looks like? Or where he resides?'

'Yes. He is a bald-headed, portly man of middle age, and he lives in Sheen Street.'

'In that case, it is surely just a matter of informing the police.'

'Unfortunately, Clarissa, it is not that simple. In the eyes of the Law, Lipsius is a respectable citizen. One needs proof in order to arrest a man, and Lipsius is so infernally cunning that proof is almost impossible to find. What good would it do were I to inform the police about what Lipsius does to the unfortunate children whom he buys in the East End? He disposes of the bodies after he has used them for his foul purposes. As for the wretched parents who sold them to him, they did so to avoid starvation, and I acquired their story only because I was prepared to be more liberal than Lipsius with my money. Insofar as the police are concerned, their lips are sealed; one does not confess repulsive crimes to one's worst enemies. As for the whores that disappear, who cares about them? The Madams who sold them would obviously deny the story. Then there are certain robberies and murders in which I see the hand of Lipsius, but that is because I am familiar with his style. I cannot imagine a police inspector putting up with me talking about style for one moment. The Order has some little proof that Lipsius celebrates the Black Mass and other more dangerous impieties, but I fear that the Law would merely regard me as a lunatic were I to bring this to its attention.'

'So what can you do?'

'Precious little, apart from wait. I hope that in

the not too distant future, Lipsius will make a mistake which will enable me to pounce upon my prey, yet I must admit that I am far from being optimistic.' He sighed and fell silent.

'There's something more,' said Clarissa. 'I can feel it.'

'Correct again. But it is in a sense so trivial an occurrence, that I do not know whether or not I should ascribe any importance to it. Except that . . .'

'Except that your intuition tells you that you should,' finished Clarissa. 'That is enough of excuses. Your port is like liquid velvet, and your hashish has made me tingle all over. I desire nothing more at present than to recline lazily upon this sofa and let your words caress me and conjure up strange scenes within my mind.'

Renshawe stubbed out his cigarette, while Clarissa stretched herself upon the couch like some great and supple cat.

'A request like that cannot possibly be ignored,' said Renshawe. 'Very well. Yesterday evening I was feeling somewhat depressed, and even an hour's meditation proved of no avail. I therefore decided to take a long walk beneath the flaming gas-lamps that add so much charm to this great city, and set off along the pavement, very deep in thought. At length I found myself in that garishly illuminated street we call the Strand, mingling with and being jostled by the crowds that throng there in search of some pleasurable diversion. I wandered along for a few minutes, appreciating this distraction from my gloomy thoughts, then noticed the entrance to a restaurant. It struck me that I had had no dinner, and since the place seemed crowded and cheerful, I resolved to enter.

'I seated myself at a corner table and proceeded to enjoy a three-course dinner washed down by a bottle of most acceptable claret. As I was about to call for the bill, my attention was distracted by the behaviour of a young woman who had just entered. She was quite a handsome lady, with tresses of flaming red hair, but what made her behaviour so noticeable was the fact that she seemed quite panic-stricken. She stood just inside the entrance, wholly oblivious to the attention she was attracting, and glancing around her in a manner that suggested pure dread. It was as though a hare had paused for one moment, only to hear in the distance the baying of slavering hounds, and her eyes were wide with terror. I thought of rising to ask if I could be of any assisance, when suddenly she glanced behind her, out of the plate-glass window, at which point her jaw sagged, and she turned so fearfully pale, I thought the poor woman would faint. Then she ran right through the restaurant and into the doorway marked ''Private'' and I hoped for her sake that there existed a back entrance.

'Just as she vanished, a bulky man in an ill-fitting coat stormed into the restaurant, and stood

there panting and fuming. He was an ugly individual, with a ginger moustache that grew into a pair
of bulbous chin-whiskers. He stared around the
restaurant, and I shivered at what I saw. Rarely
can such fury have clouded a human face, all the
more frightful for its semblance of control. Were a
demon to arise in the midst of Man, it could not
have conveyed the inhuman fury that raged beneath human flesh. With an ugly oath, he turned
and tore from the restaurant and out into the crowd,
with something in his eyes that was viler even than
murder.

'I lost no time in paying my bill, and dashed out
into the Strand, but my small delay had rendered
me incapable of finding him. I returned to the
restaurant and asked the manager if there was a
back entrance. For a sovereign he told me that
there was, and a lady had astonished his cooks by
fleeing past them and out into the back streets only
a few moments before. He allowed me to leave by
this entrance, but there was no trace of her at all.
My only recourse was to hail a cab and return
home. Now, Clarissa,' he poured himself a liberal
quantity of brandy, 'it is hardly a convincing
conclusion, but an incident like that reminded me
irresistibly of Lipsius. I have no proof, nor even a
clue, nothing beyond a mental association. I have
imagined the situation many times today, and there
was about it something so horrible that I cannot ex-

plain it in any of the ordinary ways. Do you see what I mean?'

Clarissa's eyes were closed. For a moment she saw the crowded restaurant, then the fear of an unknown woman, and the rage of an unknown man, and it was as if the gates of Hell had abruptly opened to belch forth the smoke of evil passions which never can be slaked and which stalked the streets of London before her frightened eyes, and then the vision was gone.

'Yes,' she said quietly. 'I do see.'

'And yet,' Renshawe continued, 'when all is said and done, it remains but a glimpse of some private inferno, and little will be achieved by further speculation. If I am meant to see more, I shall see more; otherwise it will remain a bizarre and frightening adventure without meaning, and disappear into the darkness from which it erupted. Over its development we cannot exercise any form of supervision or control, so let us speak of more pleasant and immediate matters. How long can you stay?'

'My servants have been instructed to say that I am suffering from one of my frequent attacks of indisposition, and that I am not expected to recover until tomorrow afternoon. A carriage will call for me shortly before lunch.'

'An enchanting arrangement, Clarissa. Allow me to take you on a tour of my new dwelling. I think you will compliment me on the manner in which I have furnished the bed-chamber. It is hung entirely with mirrors.'

'That,' Clarissa murmured, 'is hardly an un-pleasing prospect. Pray begin Charles. I could not wish for a better guide. I trust you will find me an able and willing student.'

2

The Encounter of the Hansom Cabs

(The Man in the Stove-pipe Hat)

Lady Clarissa Mountford was a woman who throughly enjoyed the maximum of formality provided that beneath it there boiled and seethed the minimum of restraint. This combination had been admirably served by Mr Charles Renshawe, and it was with the smile of a cat who has just enjoyed a vat of cream that she kissed him goodbye and descended the stairs of the Bloomsbury flat to her carriage.

Since it was Autumn, she had ordered the closed brougham rather than the open victoria, and it was with a sigh of contentment that she sank back into the cusions and lit a Turkish cigarette. Really, she thought, it was quite ridiculous that a woman could only smoke a cigarette in private, yet at the same time, the convention made the act seem delightfully wicked and thereby imparted spice to the commonplace. It reminded her of the occasions when she had defended the institution of marriage on the grounds that it lent so much exictement to the pleasures of adultery.

Clarissa was an exception to her class not so

much in her behaviour as in her way of thinking. She knew full well that the secret of happiness lies simply in appreciating what one has, and she appreciated every smallest one of the privileges to which her wealth and social station entitled her. She had no patience with those bored lady aristocrats who languidly declared that only the poor were noble, realising full well that poverty is honourable only to the rich and useless. At the same time she never allowed her good fortune to disturb her. She acquiesced in the fact that it was unfair, but believed this to be part of the human condition. Although she admired the work of a disreputable dramatist by the name of Bernard Shaw, she nevertheless felt that if the rich did precious little good with their wealth, this could not compare with the harm governments might do when possessed of it.

For Clarissa money could buy two invaluable things: freedom and pleasure. She was thankful for her own good fortune, and was determined to use it. She saw clearly enough the corruption of the system in which they all lived, but felt that this system was the product of human beings, and could not be changed for the better until human beings had changed for the better. It had then been her resolution to make a start by changing herself.

As previously related, she had felt prompted to search for the wisdom enshrined in the ancient mysteries. For one unused to self-discipline, the quest had been a hard one. She had had to learn how to develop and control her body, imagination, mind, emotions and will, and how to make them fit vehicles for the reception of the Light. Ultimately she had made more than a little progress, but she remained painfully aware of how much was still to be done.

Clarissa threw her cigarette out of the window and coolly regarded the streets through which she travelled. The brougham had left the abode of affluent aficionadoes of the arts that was Bloomsbury far behind, and the horses were now cantering along the Mall towards the Palace before beginning their leisured trot in the direction of Kensington. With a certain measure of contempt, Clarissa noted the eighteenth-century livery of some of the other drivers and footmen who were taking their mistresses for their midmorning ride; it was only the tasteless and vulgar who displayed such crass ostentation.

She had just decided to fix her sparkling eyes upon the pageant of dark green and gold and russet brown that was the tapestry of St. James's Park when she was abruptly recalled from her reverie by the sound of galloping hooves. Immediately she peered out of the right-hand window to see a hansom cab about to draw level. For one brief moment its passenger could be glimpsed, a young woman of handsome appearance with flaming red hair. Then a whip cracked repeatedly and a horse which foamed at the mouth from its exertions raced by, and the cab shot off into the distance.

It was certainly unusual for a London cabman to set so spanking a pace. Clarissa looked back and saw yet another hansom kicking up the dust and leaves with its spinning wheels. It was only then that her mind whipped back to Renshawe's story of the previous evening.

She leaned out of the window once more to inspect the pursuing cab, and could distinguish a man as the sole passenger, though she could not make out his features. The vehicle was approaching fast, and Clarissa thereupon decided to interfere with the course of this unusual chase.

'Burroughs!' she called to her driver. 'The cab behind us! Do not let it pass!'

Instantly the horses accelerated. Clarissa heard the clatter of the hooves behind her draw nearer, until it seemed that the cab would draw abreast of the carriage, and she could discern the ginger moustache and chin-whiskers of the pursuer, who hid his eyes beneath the crown of an ill-fitting top-hat. Two horses, however, proved speedier than one, and the next moment the brougham drew away, cut the corner which led into the area before Buckingham Palace, and plungd insanely onward along the Buckingham Palace Road. Clarissa looked back to see that she had considerably outdistanced the pursuing hansom, one of the wheels of which looked extremely unsteady. At the top of the road it halted,

and a violent altercation between cabman and passenger could just be made out.

'Stop!' she cried to her driver, and the brougham
slowed to a shuddering halt, which consumed a
hundred yards. Clarissa stared back to see the
hansom driving off, and the passenger making a
fearful exhibition of himself. He appeared to be
dancing with rage upon the public pavement.

'This singular lack of self-control,'' Clarissa muttered to herself, 'is really quite deplorable.'

Now the man sighted the stationary brougham
which had been the cause of his discomfiture, and
set off along the pavement in the manner of General Gordon of Khartoum. As he came closer, it
looked as though he was grinding his teeth, and
despite the chill wind, he perspired as if with
righteous indignation. Clarissa awaited his arrival
with considerable expectation, for she enjoyed few
things more than unexpected adventure. As he
drew nearer, she was able to make out what manner of man he was, and she recoiled at the
unsightliness of the picture he presented. Although
expensively dressed, his apparel was nevertheless
curiously ill-suited, and worn without grace or
bearing. It was with little aesthetic pleasure that
she perceived his beady brown eyes and pasty
complexion, yet it was in a mood of anticipation
that she composed herself as he drew alongside
and glared into the interior of the carriage.

'Pardon me, Madam,' he rasped, after clearing

41

his throat in a most inelegant manner, 'but I feel obliged to point out to you that your inexplicable behaviour has placed the lives of the citizens of London in very grave danger.'

'Sir, if you can inform me on what authority you yourself risk the lives and limbs of these citizens you speak of by so hazardous and negligent a chase,' Clarissa riposted coolly, 'I should be most grateful. In another and more gracious age, your singular lack of courtesy for those who have the misfortune to use the highway in close proximity to yourself would have been justly rewarded by a whipping.'

'Madam!' fumed the man, 'with all possible respect that is due to your station, you are in no position to know the full circumstances of what has transpired. I cannot but do my duty as a citizen, and point out to you that your conduct may have dire consequences, which I am sure that you as a sensible lady, will regret deeply.'

'As you so directly point out, sir, I have no knowledge of the motives which may have impelled your outrageous display,' Clarissa responded, 'but since the result has been so lamentably uncivilised, I am not at all sure if I desire to be enlightened.'

'I see it is no use,' the man muttered, lowering his eyes, and allowing his shoulders to slump. 'Certainly I could explain that my motives are nothing if not right-minded and eminently respectable, but I see to my cost that I cannot hope for the smallest measure of understanding for the impossible task upon which I am engaged.' He turned away, a veritable portrait of misery.

'Wait!' Clarissa commanded. The man's head shot round with, she thought, quite sufficient alacrity. 'It appears from what you say that I may have done you an injustice. If you will step into my carriage one moment, I shall be pleased to hear your explanation for this altogether extraordinary escapade.'

Although the ginger-bearded gentleman looked anything but salubrious company, Clarissa felt no alarm as he mounted the carriage steps. Her Ladyship's gloved hand was deep within her handbag, where her fingers fondled the loaded derringer which her father had given her as a souvenir from his days in the West of America.

'That, Madam, would be a great kindness,' the pasty-faced man was saying. 'I only hope that passers-bye will not misinterpret our conduct, vulnerable as it is before the severe eyes of the censorious.'

'Sir, if you please, that is quite enough pious humbug for today,' Clarissa said sharply. As the man stepped into the carriage, she called out: 'Burroughs! A slow and leisured trot around Hyde Park.'

'You cannot comprehend how much I appreciate your solicitiousness . . .' began the man, but was

Gerald Suster

cut off in mid-sentence by the abrupt opening of Clarissa's volumious fan.

'Sir, I desire to hear your explanation and not your pleasantries. Kindly relate your tale without undue vulgar ornament.'

'Very well, Madam,' replied the man, 'I shall do as a gracious lady bids me. My name is Henry Potter, and I am the only son of a poor but honest clergyman. The want of means has compelled me to forgo the advantages which a university education might confer, and I have been forced by circumstances to earn my daily bread by being an indispensable assistant to those whom life has blessed. This has led me into many divers kinds of employment, but for the last five years I have enjoyed the good fortune of steady and remunerative toil within the confines of the medical profession. I have held the post of assistant to Dr Sebastian Crooke, whose work with the insane has too high a reputation among the cognoscenti to warrant further comment.

'As someone so highly placed as yourself must be aware, Dr Crooke administers a private asylum for the mentally afflicted in the vicinity of Highgate Village in North West London, which is where I assist him in his invaluable labours. Since many of the patients in his care have been committed by the highest families in the land, you will understand that the need for discretion is absolute.

'Diseases of the mind are, despite the consider-

44

able advancement of our knowledge, terrain as unknown as that of the interior of South America, and the patients who inhabit our asylum are, to all intents and purposes, incurable. We have, for instance, a young girl who is the daughter of a Lord of not inconsiderable diplomatic renown, and who is afflicted by a mania which causes her to behave towards young men in a manner which I would blush to repeat. We have also a young lady whom only the surgeon's knife saved from scandal and disgrace, and who in consequence threatened to ruin the career of her very own father, an industrialist of more than European fame. I mention these instances only to impress upon you the importance of the matters with which we are called upon to deal.

Dr Crooke believes that his patients should enjoy the utmost comfort, and every courtesy befitting their social stations. The fact that his asylum is most generously endowed enables him to permit the insane a freedom which elsewhere they would be denied. Moreoever, he encourages them to express themselves in the forms of pottery, painting and writing, a practice which is, to say the least, unusually enlightened.

'The entire operation was admirable in every respect, and the doctor gave me to understand that my work merited advancement in the not too distant future. My troubles began six months ago, however, when we accepted as a patient the nephew of a prominent politician and Cabinet Minister. This nephew had churlishly rejected all the advantages which his family desired to aid him with, and instead chose to flatter himself with the delusion that he was a man of letters. Given the conspicuous immorality of literature's current self-proclaimed practitioners, this was a decision which caused his benevolent uncle acute embarrassment.

'The young man proceeded to disappear into a garret, and there indulged in vices and personal habits too shameful to be mentioned in the company of the fairer sex. It is hardly surprising that his mind soon gave way, and he found himself prey to all manner of delusion. As if this was not horrendous enough, he fell into the merciless clutches of an adventuress of the kind that all decent human beings abhor, and this vile woman chanced upon the fact that her literary poseur would soon receive a large sum of money from a trust fund which was the result of his uncle's magnanimity.

'I am sure you will agree that it was most fortunate that the whereabouts of the foolish young man were discovered before the vicious female could fasten her teeth into his innocent flesh and thereby acquire his fortune. He was found screaming one night in a single sordid room in Camden Town, quite, quite mad. His uncle wisely decided to commit him to the care of Dr Crooke, and even my venerable employer initially found it difficult to perceive the smallest semblance of sense behind the young man's ravings. His general conduct was in addition intensely distressing. One night he attacked a female patient and endeavoured to sink his teeth into her throat. Indeed, it seemed as though there was nothing we could do for him, for after a brief and perfunctory interest in writing, he displayed no desires other than for the bizarre and homicidal.

'It was a situation of the utmost sadness. Oftentimes he would howl at the moon, or else would endeavour to assault female patients in a way that put them in fear of their lives, and in terror of something else, which among decent people has not even a name.

'Dr Crooke sadly admitted that he had failed hitherto, yet persisted in his methods of kindness and consideration. He braved sights that made my blood freeze as though it was a Siberian stream in the winter months, and endured even the period when the lunatic went about upon all fours and would eat nothing but raw beef. But as he continued with his expert ministrations, it did seem that the madman's lamentable condition was at last being in some degree alleviated.

'Soon he began to walk and talk once more, and his behaviour showed signs of lucidity, tempered though it was by outbursts of murderous fury. Indeed, it was Dr Crooke's considered opinion that within three years the poor unfortunate might be fit to take his place once more among the healthy.

'Alas! This was not to be. Bitterly do I regret that night thirteen days ago when I was on duty, and responsible for the welfare of the patients from midnight until the morning. Like a fool I thought that all was well, and chose to snatch a few blissful hours of sleep. I had no means of knowing how desperate was the adventuress with whom we had to contend, for her tenacity in the matter of money must be unrivalled. For she saw her chance slipping away from her, resolved upon unscrupulous measures, and hired a gang of depraved roughs, creatures from the lowest slime of London. That night they invaded the asylum as I slept, and released the poor mad gentleman, released him before the helpless eyes of our patients. When I awoke, disturbed by the clamour, it was too late, and then the horror of what I had precipitated dawned upon me.

'Words cannot stress sufficiently the urgency of the situation. The adventuress has him in her power, and will persuade him to sign over to her his entire worldly wealth. But that is by no means the major peril. A homicidal maniac walks among us, and who knows upon whose throat his itching fingers might alight? Then think of the scandal! The family name would be dragged through the mire, and the career of his uncle would be terminated shamefully.

'No man could be more aware of this than Dr Crooke, whose unimpeachable reputation for discretion would suffer a calamitous blow. He has chosen to blame me for my negligence, and I was informed that I was to consider myself dismissed, without references, until such a time as I returned with his escaped patient. My own livelihood was now at stake, and I lost no time in setting out.

'As you may imagine, the odds against success were extraordinary. There was no one to whom I could turn, owing to the need for discretion, and at first my search proved wholly fruitless. All I had to aid me was my guess that a woman like this upstart would choose an area like Chelsea as her place of residence, and by day and by night I paced its pavements.

'I had all but given up hope and resigned myself to the thought of the remainder of my life being passed in obscurity and penury, when suddenly, this very morning, I sighted the cause of our consternation, the adventuress. I had feared that she would disguise herself, but so ruled is she by her vanity that she is incapable of hiding her tresses of flaming red hair. I immediately approached her, but she sighted me, paled, and hailed a hansom, hoping to elude my arrest. I remained undaunted by her tactic, mounted a cab myself, and clattered off in hot pursuit.

'My excitement quickened as we continued our chase through Kensington, up into Hyde Park, past

the Green Park, up Piccadilly, down through
Trafalgar Square and into the Mall. All the while I
gained upon her, and entertained hopes of seizing
my elusive quarry as we reached the Palace, but
you, Madam, for no sensible reason that I can
discern, chose to thwart my altruistic designs, and
hence smite my hopes with a thunderbolt.' And
Mr Potter hung his crestfallen head in sorrow.

'I do sympathise with your predicament, Mr
Potter,' answered Clarissa, who thought the man's
delivery a trifle pompous, 'and I have found your
story to be of considerable interest. However, I
cannot but sympathise equally with the young
man whom you describe.'

'Ah yes, the poor unfortunate,' sighed Mr Potter.
'Entirely at the mercy of a ruthless and determined
woman . . .'

'No, that is not quite what I meant. I see him as
a misunderstood and sensitive soul upon whom a
spirited woman has taken pity . . .'

'Madam!'

'Kindly do not interupt. It is an unpleasing habit.
As I was saying, Mr Potter, I have no doubt that
the young man's cruel relatives have confined him
to a madhouse in order that his tyrannical uncle
may further his vile political ambitions without
hindrance of embarrassment. You have been but
an unfortunate pawn in this sordid tragedy, Mr
Potter, and I would counsel you to seek employment at the hands of someone more worthy of your

talents than the grasping quack you describe. As for the young man, I sincerely hope that he eludes his captors, and I wish him and his lady-love, whose chivalry is equal to her devotion, every possible happiness.'

'Madam, I cannot tolerate this lamentable misconception,' Mr Potter broke in impatiently. 'You are obviously a generous soul, but I regret that your bounty is misplaced. I have upon my person a document which proves conclusively that the young man urgently requires the assistance of a specialist in mental pathology. He himself wrote the manuscript for Dr Crooke. Pray permit me to read it to you, and I am sure you will alter your opinion.'

'I am always willing to listen to fresh evidence,' said Clarissa. 'Proceed.'

At these words, Mr Potter placed a pair of small and rimless spectacles upon his red and perspiring nose, extracted a manuscript from the inside of his coat, and in a loud, hoarse voice proceeded to read the tale of:

THE MAN IN THE STOVE-PIPE HAT

'Very well, doctor, since you so obviously know best, I shall oblige. You tell me that you are "not wholly clear as to what the trouble may be". You "venture to suggest" that I write a complete account of what it is that has "disturbed" me. Ah, the gentle language of the medical profession! No doubt you will "read the account with interest".

'Of course I have little hope that you will believe it. If I really thought you would, I would indeed be as mad as all the other patients in this "home" of yours. No, no, you merely happen to think that this exercise "might help", that it might give you some insight into my regrettable "disturbance". Oh my dear doctor, you shall certainly have insight! With the wisdom of your kind, you will no doubt ignore it and label my tale the fantasy of a lunatic.

'Let me insist, however, that I will be describing actual events. You will smile, and shake your head, for these events are far beyond your own experience. But in dismissing them, as you inevitably will, you reveal not the intelligence of the true man of science, but the narrowness of the bigot.

'I have told you that I cannot bear ghost stories. Did you wonder why, dear doctor? Did you know that until recently they were my favourite form of fiction? Did you know that I had forgotten when a ghost story last perturbed me? Why, then, does the very thought of a ghostly tale now fill me with terror and foreboding? Ha! Ponder on that, my friend, and explain it if you can! You are very fond of explaining things.

'Yes, once I loved tales of horror and of the supernatural, and not, I repeat, because they frightened me. It was the atmosphere of these stories that appealed, and the momentary glimpse into the bizarre world of the creator's mind. Obviously I did not believe the stories to be true, or even possible. I agreed with other ''reasonable men'' that that which cannot be measured, does not exist. Ghosts cannot be measured, therefore ghosts do not exist.

'My interest in these tales was therefore of a psychological nature, and I admit I have always been fascinated by the mind's more macabre depths. I admired too the literary skill with which masters of the genre symbolised the anxieties within us, and projected these symbols into a well-wrought piece of fiction.

'Given my interest in, and admiration for the genre, and given my resolve to become a writer, it is not surprising that I eventually decided to try my hand at writing a tale of the supernatural. After six weeks, I produced several stiff and crippled abortions. There was a tale of a man who was haunted by himself as he would be; another of a man visited in his dreams by a beautiful succubus, who left him ''a white, a shrivelled slug-like thing''; another of a professor of marine biology, who evoked the Fish-God, and then began to notice on his skin the creeping presence of green scales. Not bad, I suppose, for an amateur's first attempts, but that was all that could be said in their favour. Even I could recognise that some vital element was lacking, and that vital element was atmosphere.

'I spent many hours of prolonged thought in examining this question, and came to the conclusion that what we call "atmosphere" is produced by the writer's consciousness of horror, the horror of our world being upset by beings which know not our laws of logic and science. Only a writer who has experienced this can convey the element of spiritual terror to his readers. My stories had failed because I had never felt this fright, and instead manipulated symbols which I knew nothing of. In short, I lacked inspiration.

'Of course, inspiration is not something which one can command. It comes, or it does not come, but some environments are more welcome to its visitation than others. That is why the ensuing Saturday morning found me idling in a musty Bloomsbury bookshop, near the Charing Cross Road. I was in search of the strange, and this dim room lined by dusty shelves of old and mouldering books possessed something of the eerie about it.

'This shop, I surmised, was known to seekers after the curious, for it contained shelves of strange and forbidden books, and was peopled by customers who prowled restlessly between them like beings possessed. Feverish and glittering eyes regarded me, and I hastily stumbled over to a section at the back and pretended to be absorbed in studying the titles that reposed there.

'I could feel several pairs of eyes probing my neck as I regarded rows of abhorred volumes, whose existence my reading had only hinted at. There was *The Greater Key of Solomon*, Aptolcater's *Book of Power*, *The Grimoire of the Red Dragon*, the *Unaussprechlichen Kulten* of von Juntz, and the Comte D'Erlette's *Culte des Ghoules*, among other obscure works. A smell as of stale and sickly incense lingered in the air around those books, and I began to feel slightly uncomfortable.

' ''Yes . . .'' whispered a croaking voice behind me, and I started. It was the owner of the shop, a short, wizened man, whose white hair straggled from his scalp in grimy tufts. ''Can I help you?''

'The customers were still peering at me, and my discomfort increased. I felt hot, unnaturally hot, and oppressed by the lack of air. I think it must have been that which prompted my next action, for as the room began to swim before my watering eyes, I snatched a book at random from the shelf.

' ''How much?'' I enquired, and my voice also emerged as a parched whisper. He stared at the volume I held.

' ''Ah, *De Vermis Mystriis* by Ludwig van Prinn,'' he croaked, and added with an evil chuckle, ''a rare and interesting work, very interesting . . . and the price is a mere five pounds.''

'Unaccountably desperate to be gone, I thrust the money into his shrivelled hand, and ran from the shop into the refreshing gusts of wind that swept the street outside. It was only then that I realised that I had parted with a considerable sum in exchange for something which I did not particularly want. Yet despite my considerable irritation, not even the loss of one hundred pounds would have induced me to re-enter that sinister sanctum of the esoteric.

'I returned to my attic room, brewed a pot of strong tea, and sat down to study my involuntary purchase. That stale sickly smell of the shop still clung to the worn black buckram binding, upon which the title was stamped in gold Gothic letters. My room was light and quite cheerful, and I turned the pages with some little curiosity.

'I have had the good fortune to be blessed with a first-class classical education, and so found no difficulty in translating from the Latin. The title page informed me that *Of the Mysteries of the Worm* was ''composed'' by Ludwig van Prinn as a result of his ''experiments and divers researches'', and privately published in Amsterdam in 1862. The frontispiece consisted of an etching of the author. Rarely have I regarded a visage more unpleasant, and it was with the prickling of goose-flesh that I noted it to be a self-portrait.

'Beneath the stove-pipe hat which some gentlemen affected at this period, two small staring eyes emanated malevolence from the page, a malevolence fortified by the sharp straight nose, and a pair of cruelly curving thin lips. It was a face with all the coldness of a cobra, a face which could regard a scene of torture with a smile. I shivered, and hastily turned the page.

'The contents of *Of the Mysteries of the Worm* were certainly curious. There was a preface exhorting the utmost care in the use of the spells to follow, spells so potent that to speak the words aloud might result in fearful danger to the ill-equipped and unprepared. Three chapters followed: "Of the Opening of the Gateways of Matter", "Of the Opening of the Gateways of Space and Time", and "Of the Attainment of Immortality". I could make little of these, consisting as they did for the most part of incantations in some long-forgotten barbarous tongue. Ignoring the warning of Ludwig van Prinn, I pronounced certain phrases, and of course nothing happened. Smiling at my own foolishness, I turned to the Epilogue, a brief paragraph in which van Prinn proclaimed the singular fact that he had attained immortality, and offered The Grace of the Worm to those whose aspiration was similar.

'I closed the volume and admitted to myself that it had imparted to me a sense of disquiet. It was obviously the scribbling of a madman, but there is nothing comforting about insanity. I washed up my teacup, and even as it was deluged by cold tap-water, I felt upon my skin a hot, prickling sensation. I told myself not to be so foolish. What harm could the jottings of a dead madman do to me? As an act of bravado, I seized *De Vermis Mysteriis,* flung it open, and bellowed out the gibberish that greeted my eyes. Although I remained convinced that it was all nonsense, I nevertheless continued to feel restless.

'Two hours later, the feeling had not abated, and it was then that I hit upon a remarkable idea. Only a day before I had been reproaching myself for lack of atmosphere in my stories, and now a certain small consciousness of horror was coming to birth within me. Here at last was the stimulus and inspiration which I so desperately required!

'I seized pen and paper and began to write. The story on which I laboured now possessed roots in my own experience. It concerned a writer who visited a queer bookshop in order to provoke inspiration for the tale of horror he desired to pen. There, like myself, he purchased Ludwig van Prinn's *De Vermis Mysteriis*, and in the course of reading it, he muttered aloud the forbidden incantations. As a result of those dread words, the ghost of van Prinn arose from its corpse's slumbers, and stalked into his life. The tale was narrated by the writer to that perennial ghost-story figure, ''the doctor'', and was entitled ''The Man in the Stove-pipe Hat''.

'As closely as I could, I based the tale upon my own experience. I even had my writer writing, as I was, a story entitled ''The Man in the Stove-pipe Hat''. At this point I introduced my element of horror. For as my writer scribbled, he sensed the presence of someone or something behind him, looming over his left shoulder . . .

'As I described that very scene, I too began to feel the presence of something malevolent, intensely cold and evil just behind my left shoulder.

'I jerked my head round. I saw nothing. I stared at the sentence I had just written. Then I scribbled another sentence describing what had just occurred.

' "Don't be silly," I said aloud. "It's only a story."

'Immediately I felt compelled to jot down that very sentence.

'I was now profoundly shaken. Even as my writer wondered, and made *his* writer wonder what manner of being he had brought into the world, so did I stare around my room in fearful apprehension. I, my character, and his character were feverishly telling ourselves that this was only a story. I found myself speculating as to whether I was merely a character in the story of another, and giving that thought to my own creation.

'And now I sat at my desk in a state of acute anxiety. In vain I tried to calm myself. For the tale of "The Man in the Stove-pipe Hat" seemed no longer an idea, but a monster. As I worked on it, so did my writer, and so did his writer, who, as he wrote "The Man in the Stove-pipe Hat", engendered yet another writer, and so on to infinity. An infinite number of writers wrote an infinite number of unfinished tales entitled "The Man in the Stove-pipe Hat" as if imprisoned in an eternal corridor of mirrors, and all quivered with the apprehension of the original creator, myself.

'I rose and poured myself a very stiff whisky, swallowed it in one gulp, and vowed not to continue. Instantly I was possessed by an urge to put that into my story, and within seconds, an infinite number of writers were downing an infinite number of stiff whiskies, and vowing not to continue. But what now? I paced up and down my room, plagued by the sensation that something, though I did not know what, was in the room with me, forcing upon me an irresistible urge to continue with my tale. Surely this was preferable to pacing backwards and forwards in this dim and eerie silence!

'I obeyed the urge. But I did not like the way in which my story took shape. I sent my character to bed, and gave him nightmares, and the first nightmare had him back at his desk, writing the tale of "The Man in the Stove-pipe Hat". I lost control of the events which streamed from my now fertile pen. He had nightmares of nightmares, and nightmares of nightmares of nightmares, and all involved him in sitting at his desk writing the tale of "The Man in the Stove-pipe Hat". And then came that moment in the darkness when he turned his head, and saw, standing just behind him, the figure of van Prinn, lumps of rotting flesh hanging from his face, pulpy gums bared in a parody of a mocking grin, and beady eyes glaring balefully and exuding an unfathomable evil, and at that moment I threw down my pen, and turned and saw . . . I flung myself from my chair and screamed.

'I must have swooned from fear. When I came to, it was an hour later, and there was nothing in the room save that smell of stale and sickly incense. My body was drenched in icy perspiration. I was barely conscious, numb, exhausted. Hardly aware of the movements of my limbs, I staggered to my bed and collapsed into it, to lose consciousness of one nightmare and to drift into another, and another, and another—nightmares within nightmares, writing over and over again the tale of "The Man in the Stove-pipe Hat", each nightmare culminating in that instant when I turned and saw and screamed, and tumbled into yet another tale of "The Man in the Stove-pipe Hat".

'That is how your people found me, doctor, screaming without cessation. Now you say that I am mad. Dear doctor, I would that I were. It would be an all too easy escape from the eternal recurrence of the tale of "The Man in the Stove-pipe Hat". You call me mad because you will not accept what I saw, and saw as clearly as any sane man might, and still see now as I scream for pen and paper. Why, even that mark upon my wrist you dismiss as being self-inflicted.

'But then, dear doctor, you did not see what I saw, and I saw what even my writers failed to see. *They* saw merely the hideous face of the man in the stove-pipe hat who strained after immortality.

'I saw that face attached to the great lunging body of a white and leprous coffin-worm.'

'And this man,'' Mr Potter finished impressively as he folded the manuscript and replaced it within his coat, 'now walks among us unrestrained.'

'What a bizarre and uniquely unpleasant tale!' exclaimed Clarissa. 'I do not think I would care to encounter its author. He sounds a most peculiar individual. Now I shall have nightmares.'

'Madam, I suffer them every time I fall asleep with the knowledge that he is free. But I see that I have taken up more than enough of your time, and I only hope that you will no longer think unkindly of me.'

Before Clarissa could reply, Mr Potter had opened the carriage door, and leapt out into the street.

'Farewell, Madam, and thank you,' he called out as the brougham left him behind, then he shrugged his shoulders and disappeared in the direction of the Albert Memorial.

Clarissa waved briefly as he receded from view, then ordered Burroughs to take her home. Mr

Potter's queer tale had certainly disturbed her, but this was not entirely due to its content. She had not liked the irritating manner of the narrator, and felt that there was about him some indefinable element of repulsion. His story had been nothing if not astonishing, but she could not help wondering if she believed a word of it.

3

The Incident of the Gentleman Attacked by Footpads

(Many Spaces and a Time)

It was a drab and rainy afternoon when Charles Renshawe set off for one of his frequent solitary walks. He had not seen Clarissa for three days, during which time his mind had been occupied by thoughts of Dr Lipsius, and by the episode in the restaurant which he had witnessed, and he now felt that a stroll in the chill damp air might clarify the maze of his thoughts. To his intense disappointment, he had seen nothing of either the lady with flaming red hair or her pursuer, and at times he found himself feeling cheated of a clue.

One could be pardoned for thinking of Renshawe as an idle man of the leisured classes. Certainly he made no effort to convince anyone that he was anything else. This was quite deliberate, for it enabled him to attend to his work in the guise of an innocuous dilettante, hence effectively camouflaging its true nature. For Renshawe had decided to devote his life to the search for what some ·call ecstasy, and others call God. Many years of obscure studies, hazardous travels, and arcane disciplines had led to that glorious instant in which he had received a vision of the Universe, and saw inscribed therein the luminous image of the Creator. Since that time, as a member of a secret Fraternity which had endured for many hundreds of years, he had aspired to further his knowledge of the Light, and upon attaining to Adeptship, had sworn the oath of obligation to do battle with Darkness in whatever form he found it.

The battles which he fought were for the most part not the kind that are reported in our daily newspapers, but concerned the issues behind the news that most believed. The public learned of their consequences only through reading of the odd fatal accident or inexplicable suicide. Renshawe had himself been close to death on many occasions, but hitherto had always ultimately emerged victorious.

Now he hunted for Lipsius, that monster of countless crimes against the human soul, wrapped in a net of caution and corruption, and aided by loyal and able assistants. Renshawe had caught glimpses of his doings but the dread doctor always eluded his grasp, and continued to present to society the beaming and benevolent face of a solid and respectable citizen.

Such were Renshaw's thoughts as he trod the Tottenham Court Road, proceeded north into Hampstead Road, then turned off into a mean and shabby side-street. The rain spattered his cape and broad-brimmed hat as he strolled along the wet, leaf-littered pavement, swinging his sword-stick, and speculating momentarily as to what type of person inhabited these grimy dwelling-places, for the streets were quite deserted.

As he turned a corner by an open railway tunnel, he espied about one hundred yards ahead something that recalled a ballet. A tall gentleman dressed in a high silk hat and in what looked like a fur-trimmed coat was swinging his walking-stick in an endeavour to fend off three ruffians armed with truncheons. In and out the footpads danced, deftly avoiding his blows, and the dull raps of wood upon wood echoed in the empty road. Although he failed to harm his assailants, the gentleman was giving an excellent account of himself, out-numbered as he was. An abrupt cry broke the silence of the violent dance, then the victim fell to the pavement. Instantly the ruffians were upon him, kicking him, and thwacking his prone form with their weapons.

Renshawe did not lose a moment in rushing to his assistance. As he ran, he drew the sword which lay concealed within his cane, and brandished it in the air. The rogues paused in their assault; one of them pointed at the steel blade in Renshawe's hand; then with a departing kick at their intended victim, all three scattered into the alleyways with which the street connected, vanishing as Renshawe reached the battered gentleman, who was endeavouring to rise and dust himself off. Though his coat was dusty and dishevelled, he seemed almost entirely unharmed.

'A thousand thanks for your timely aid, my dear sir,' said this smooth, smiling and clean-shaven gentleman. 'Your arrival could not have occurred at a more opportune moment. Allow me to introduce myself. Sedgemoor is the name, Harold Sedgemoor, and I am greatly indebted to your promptitude and courage.'

'Renshawe, Charles Renshawe, and very glad to make your acquaintance. I admired the stoutness with which you defended your person.' They shook hands warmly. 'But I must confess my astonishment at the boldness of these foot-pads! To attack a man in broad daylight! This is hardly a disreputable area, despite its outward semblance of unremitting shabbiness.'

'Not so long ago I would have been as astonished as your good self, Mr Renshawe,' Mr Sedgemoor replied, 'but now I am only too well aware of the origins of this murderous attack. No longer is London a safe city for me, for I know to my cost that they will stop at nothing.'

' "They"?' Renshawe queried. 'Surely you are not alleging that there exists some form of conspiracy against you, Mr Sedgemoor?'

'I deeply regret that I am,' the man answered. 'That however, is a very long tale, and I do not wish to weary you with its exposition. No doubt you have urgent matters which call for your attendance, and I have detained you long enough.'

'On the contrary, I find what you say absorbing. Indeed, I would appreciate it if you could spare the time to relate your story to me. I live not far from here. We could take a cab, and enjoy a little refreshment.'

'That is most civil of you, Mr Renshawe,' returned the other, 'I must be away by six, but I am otherwise at your service. Dear me, it seems that my walking stick is damaged beyond repair. I shall leave it here, and purchase another tomorrow morning. One just like your own, I think. It is a splendid weapon. Does it accompany you everywhere?'

'Yes, always.'

'A very wise precaution, if I may say so. One cannot be too careful these days. Ah, I do believe I see a cab.'

Fifteen minutes later they were sipping malt whisky in Renshawe's flat.

'I see you live well, Mr Renshawe,' remarked Mr Sedgemoor, who had kept up a ceaseless stream of conversation from the moment that they had taken the hansom. 'It is the only way to live. May I commend your taste in art? It is very rare these days that one encounters such choice refinement. You see, I myself am a scholar and man of letters, and it distresses me how vulgar our culture has become. Take literature, for example, which is my own field. Ever since the lamentable disgrace of Mr Oscar Wilde, standards have fallen to a level that would disgrace even the Americans, and we are deluged by works which are either disagreeably sensational or dismally platitudinous.'

'My sentiments exactly, Mr Sedgemoor, with the exception of your strictures concerning the Americans. The United States is indeed a young nation with little cultural heritage, but the Americans I have met have been perfectly charming.'

'Then you have been more fortunate than myself. But to return to the question of literature, are you at all acquainted with the work of an author by the name of Septimus Keen?'

'No, I have not experienced that particular pleasure.'

'A pleasure it certainly is, Mr Renshawe, but your statement does not surprise me. Mr Keen's work has not yet seen publication, and is known only to a handful of admirers, of whom I am one. Unfortunately, my devotion to his work has resulted in considerable personal risk.'

'How so, Mr Sedgemoor? I am familiar with the ineptitude of the gentlemen who currently pose as literary critics, but surely they would not stoop to the assassination of your reputation in the world of letters as a result of your laudable devotion to the work of an obscure writer?'

'No, even they would not stoop to conduct so base,' sighed Mr Sedgemoor, 'yet even that would be preferable to losing my life, which is the prospect that currently confronts me. Permit me to explain. I first encountered Septimus Keen about a year ago in a public house in Hampstead. I liked him immensely, and upon learning that he occupied himself with the pursuit of literature, I persuaded him to let me see some examples of his work. It is not often that a scholar like myself is privileged to discover a talent which savours strongly of genius, but that is precisely what occurred. I could barely contain my excitement over finding work that was unrivalled for its fertility of imagination. I am not entirely without influence in the world of letters, and I envisaged the publication of his tales with an introductory essay from my own pen, as being a literary event of the first magnitude.

'I put my proposal to him,' Mr Sedgemoor continued, 'and he assented. We therefore started work upon preparing a manuscript for publication, and during that time I learned more of this remarkable individual. He is the newphew of a prominent member of Lord Salisbury's Government, who has chosen to reject the advantages which his illustrious family desired to confer upon him, in favour of the honourable pursuit of literature. It is deeply regrettable that this decision has aroused the mortal emnity of his uncle, whose name discretion forbids me to mention. Six months ago, I learned to my horror and amazement that Septimus Keen, as we shall call him, had been rudely seized by his uncle's agents, and incarcerated in a private asylum. I am sad to say that my most diligent enquiries failed to elicit the whereabouts of the cell in which the young writer undoubtedly languished. I did all I could to obtain an interview with his uncle, hoping to reason with him, but experienced nothing but failure.

'Bitterly did I resign myself to this catastrophe, consoled only by the fact that I possessed certain of Mr Keen's manuscripts. I resolved to have these published at no matter what cost. I did not realise that Fate had yet another heavy blow in store for me. Seven days ago, I received an unexpected visitor. She was a striking young woman who would not reveal her name, and whose speech was brief and peremptory. She informed me that I was meddling in matters that were not my concern, and thus placing myself in grave danger. I learned that Septimus Keen had escaped from the asylum with her assistance, and was now in her care. She gave me to understand that some nefarious form of espionage lay behind these events, and that I must hand over all the manuscripts of Septimus Keen, or else place myself in dire physical peril. I dislike being threatened, and no one has ever accused me of cowardice, and so I refused to accede to her request. Her departing words chilled me to the marrow:

' "If you will not co-operate with me, Mr Sedgemoor, I shall have to take steps to ensure your compliance. The next time I see you, it will be to contemplate your corpse.''

'Before I could recover my composure, the infernal woman had departed, and since that time, I have lived in fear. I have suffered two assaults and an attempted burglary, and today I was saved only by your timely intervention. What do you think, Mr Renshaw? Is not my situation a distressing one?'

'Most distressing, Mr Sedgemoor. Have you sought the protection of the police?'

'No, for I fear that they would not believe me. I am all confusion at present, calm though I superficially appear. Each time I venture abroad, my eyes search the streets, and I dread lest I witness the flaming red hair of the vile woman.'

'Flaming red hair, Mr Sedgemoor?' cried Renshawe. 'This is really quite extraordinary, for I have seen a lady answering to this description. It happened only a few days ago, in a crowded restaurant in the Strand. However, she did not strike me as being the vicious female you have described. She looked completely petrified, as though she was fleeing from some evil man. I caught a glimpse of him also, and he was a most unappetising individual. She escaped, but I do not know how the chase ended.'

'What an astonishing coincidence!' exclaimed Mr Sedgemoor. 'We are probably speaking of two different individuals, though I would be surprised if anyone bore a close resemblance to the lady I have met. I suppose it is possible that you did indeed see her, and glimpsed an incident in the frightful game of espionage, yet I cannot know for sure, and feel utterly bemused and perplexed. I do not desire to lose my life, which is pleasant, and yet I feel compelled to defend the integrity of literature.'

'Is the work of Septimus Keen important enough to warrant your risk?' enquired Renshawe, who was every bit as puzzled as his visitor claimed to be.

'My dear sir, as a gentleman of obvious education and refinement, I am sure you appreciate the need I feel to preserve the pristine purity of our culture heritage. May I say a few words in praise of the merits of Septimus Keen?'

'By all means,' Renshawe answered as he filled a long churchwarden pipe with his favourite mixture of cavendish, latakia and perique soaked in rum. 'You have my undivided attention.'

Mr Sedgemoor pulled a pile of manuscripts from his coat pocket and inspected them.

'It is difficult to know where to begin,' he remarked thoughtfully. 'Here, for instance, are two admirable detective stories. One opens with the butler bending over his master's corpse with his hand clutching the knife that has been plunged into the latter's heart. The police arrest him on the charge of murder. A private investigator decides that the situation is altogether too plausible to be believed, and begins a search for the true culprit. Every clue, however, points remorselessly to the butler, and every other suspect is possessed of a cast-iron alibi. On the last page, the investigator comes regretfully to the conclusion that the criminal was the butler. The story is entitled: 'It Was the Butler''.

'The second tale is called ''Forever a Mystery'', and here we are shown a murder which baffles both the police and the narrator. All investigations prove to be futile. The last two lines are brilliant: '' 'If it wasn't Colonel Sinclair, then who was it?' I asked. 'You may well ask,' replied the inspector.'' Masterly, quite masterly. Then here is a narrative of two men who see each other once a week for ten years simply in order to take wine together. Never at any time do these two gentlemen speak so much as a word to one another. They merely drink wine in silence. One day, one murders the other. The Burgundy was corked. And this is a tale of a man who believes that everyone he knows is united in a conspiracy against him. They are. He ends his days in a lunatic asylum. Extraordinary, quite extraordinary! You do not look entirely convinced, Mr Renshawe. We shall soon see to that. Here,' he selected another manuscript, 'your immediate persual will not cause you any regret.'

Renshawe took the manuscript from Mr Sedgemoor, and began to read the tale of:

MANY SPACES AND A TIME

'Time puzzles. I can only present the facts. Writers love to dress fiction in the guise of fact; I will put on fact the garb of fiction. The events will remain the same, but the shape will be moulded. Fiction is the arranging of events in a pattern.

'So to the story: Henry Cloves was an impecunious gentleman who lived in what was still the outskirts of London in the mid eighteenth century. In the ordinary sense of the word, he achieved nothing, and in consequence, little is known about him. According to Parish Records, he was born on June 3rd 1722 at Aston, Bucks. Beyond that, and the date of his death, knowledge of him is obscure.

'I have in my possession a document allegedly written by Cloves entitled "Record of a Curious Experiment" which I purchased from a second-hand book dealer in the Farringdon Road, and it is this work, privately printed in an edition of two hundred copies after his death, that aroused my interest in the man. It is fifty pages long, and contains also a Foreword by an anonymous friend, who may have borne the expense of publication.

'The Foreword informs us that Cloves was a gentle man of solitary habits, who remained a bachelor all his life, and who spent what little money he had on researching into the antique and the curious. This last is the only interesting facet of the Foreword, the rest being taken up with praise for the kindness and warmth of Mr Cloves, and comments on the fascination of his document. It is the work itself that demands our attention.

'In December 1781, Henry Cloves, who had all his life been preoccupied with the occult and esoteric, and who had collected all manner of jewels and figurines from the East, came upon an item of jewellery which so engrossed him, he became determined to possess it, whatever the price might be.

'The item in question was an Egyptian ankh of burnished copper, but where there should have been a space, there reposed instead a pale grey semi-precious stone, which even the dealer was unable to identify. On the ankh itself were crude but curious lines and incisions, but the stone within it was smooth and opaque.

'It was not beautiful, nor was it even particularly well-made. Nevertheless, something forced Cloves to do without his port for a month and purchase it. Perhaps it was the stone's strange pale surface, or even the enigmatic and runelike incisions.

'Cloves returned home with it, and commenced his study that very evening. It was this event which occasioned the commencement of the journal which was posthumously published as "Record of a Curious Experiment". For the very first time that Cloves stared at the stone, he fell into a curious drowsiness; a dark mist seemed to roll between himself and the object of his perception;

and then, within the stone, he saw curious scenes merging into one another. Understandably, the event confused him, and his subsequent description was not very clear: gardens formed the substance of his scenes, then merged into forests, seas and mountains. He concluded that the stone exercised an auto-hypnotic effect upon the perceiver, causing him to objectify upon it the creations of his imagination.

'From that day onwards, his journal became filled with the record of the things which he saw "in" the stone. For the most part, these corresponded with the initial experiment, and were in themselves of no particular interest. On January 18th 1781, Cloves was confronted by a series of historical scenes, but these flowed into each other too quickly for anything exact to emerge.

'On Janaury 19th, a very curious thing happened. Cloves was gazing into the stone when his attention became fixed upon a face. It was a man with grey eyes and a moustache, "dressed in outlandish garb". So intensely did this man stare at Cloves, that his presence impinged to the point of the latter feeling that he could reach out and touch him.

'We do not know why this particular vision so frightened Henry Cloves. We know that this was his last session with the ankh, that he felt himself overcome by "a mortal terror", and that the "outlandish garb" he described corresponds exactly with the coats and neck-ties worn by late-nineteenth-century man.

'It would doubtless be interesting, but fruitless, to speculate as to whether the ankh was the famous "Visionary Stone" forged by the legendary magus, Hermes Trismegistus, and mentioned by Cornelius Agrippa in his "Occult Philosophy". Was this the ankh used by the Elizabethan magician Dr John Dee to "scry in the spirit vision", as opposed to the one claimed to be his which now reposes in the British Museum? Did Sir Francis Dashwood, diabolist, acquire it in the mid-eighteenth century, hence the references to "your devilish gem" in Lord Widdicombe's letters to him? I confess that I do not know, though I suspect it to be the same stone which resulted in a sequel to the document of Henry Cloves.

'One hundred years later, a friend of mine by the name of David Tanner acquired from a penurious friend an ankh corresponding in every detail to that described by Cloves. He too was enthralled by it, and experienced a series of visions, as a result of which he commenced a record.

'On January 19th 1881, David Tanner, clerk, looked at the stone for the twenty-first time in twenty-one evenings, and saw the face of an elderly Georgian gentleman, white-wigged, who stared at him with alarming intensity. Tanner did not record how long he stared, but the event threw him into a state of acute anxiety.

'David Tanner had never heard of Henry Cloves.

'It was also the last time he ever contemplated the ankh.

'Speculation now becomes profitable. Either we are in the lap of an extraordinary coincidence, which begs an explanation for coincidence, or, through the medium of the stone, Henry Cloves and David Tanner perceived one another.

'Then let us speculate. Two people, one in 1781, and one in 1881, see each other. In different times, in different spaces, they nevertheless hold an identical object in their hands. Is the object in two places at once, or in two times at once, or are the spaces and times contained within the object?

'According to our usual view of Tiem, it was determined that Cloves should see Tanner in the future, as it was determined also that Tanner would have looked into the past. Did Time cease to operate in that instant? Or is all predicted, the past shaping the future even as the future plays its part in shaping the patterns of the past? Were I to travel back in time, my travelling back would already have happened. My travelling into the future would be the future.

'Or perhaps Henry Cloves and David Tanner were not in two times at all, but in two spaces, and everything that happens somehow happens in the present.

'That is a hard idea to grasp. It involves an

expansion of the mind that is terrifying in its vastness. I cannot do it.

'Nor, it seems, could Henry Cloves or David Tanner. They are both dead. It is easier to think that that happened in the past. And yet, I am writing about it now, and events which supposedly occurred in the past occur now in my mind, and in the mind of the reader. Everything in this story that happened in the past, is now, on these pages, occurring in the present.

2

'David Tanner's death came suddenly, on January 18th 1895. The victim of a heart-attack, he was only forty-one. I had known him quite well for several years, and so suffered some little grief. But death is inevitable, and we had never been that close, so eventually only a slight sadness remained.

'I was not surprised that he left the ankh to me in his Will, the ankh which for all I know had hastened his untimely death. I was aware of the fact that he feared the stone, and in some degree this apprehension was passed on to me. But fear is only the reverse side of the coin of curiosity, and when one goes to the end of one, one alights upon the other. That is what happened in my case, for within a week, I too was staring at the stone.

'I stared at the opaque surface, and gradually, as my eyes began to smart, a grey mist seemed to roll gently between the stone and myself. As the mist

cleared, I could see white pin-points of light dancing on the surface, and then the points of light
became stars, and the stone became night, and the
moon was waning over a dark wood.

'I was jolted by the shock of seeing this so
clearly. I started, and realised that I was sitting in
my armchair. I remember wondering whether what
I was to see had in any way been predetermined.
Then I felt myself being drawn into staring once
more.

'What occurred then is something about which it
is very difficult to write clearly. Perhaps everything which cannot be clearly expressed should be
passed over in silence, but writers are obstinate in
their battle with experience, and I am quite willing
to apply the thumbscrews to language.

'As the mists cleared once more, the pin-points
of light became the pupils of the eyes of my late
friend, David Tanner. His face was fully visible in
the stone, frowning with a manic intensity of
concentration. Then his eyes widened as he saw
me, and I recoiled, and, I could not help it, blurted
out the words: "But you're dead!" and I saw his
face whiten as the blood drained from it.

'Was it determined that this should be so, in
which case what I had done had already happened,
and all I was doing was catching up with my past,
which had lain in wait for me in the future?

'This thought whirled through my mind, and
then the picture faded and I saw another man,

dressed in the fashion of the Regency, staring at me as the whites of his eyes grew larger. I knew then where the stone was leading me, it was leading me back, or to, the spaces where others had gazed, and something in my brain buzzed to warn me of an impending insanity, but by now I was hypnotised by the ripple of faces with which I was confronted.

'They came forward and gazed and faded to be replaced by another. A malevolent old lady peered at me through her lorgnettes; a man of saturnine countenance, wearing a long, powdered wig, seemed to utter an oath as he saw me; others came and went; a Cavalier and a bucolic Jacobean, an Elizabethan courtier and a medieval astrologer, all gazed and recoiled. Faces from every space or time in what we call the last eight hundred years of history passed in quick succession before my frightened eyes. Long thin fingers descended upon the stone at certain instants as if endeavouring to shut off the vistas of speculation which had been opened.

'I am not quite sure just what occurred after that, if indeed events do occur ''after'' one another. Perhaps the stone has always existed; maybe Time does not exist within the stone; or else I was merely dreaming. Yet dreams are not without importance. When they occur, they are the only reality.

'For scenes from history passed before me in reverse. I saw the Feudal System decline into the

Dark Ages as hordes of barbarians swept through
the lands of Europe. In the Middle East, Islamic
culture was followed by Mohammed, whereupon
the Arabs became wandering nomads. The Huns
and Goths departed from the West, leaving behind
them a Roman Empire that gained in strength.

'Even faster the scenes flitted. Civilisation collapsed in Greece, to be succeeded by the cultures
of Mesopotamia, China, India and Egypt. And the
further ''back'' I travelled, the briefer became the
duration of the images. Early Man making tools
was succeeded by an Ice Age. I saw the mammoth
roam the wilds, and then pterodactyls glided through
the air as strange and monstrous reptiles crashed
and lumbered through unearthly primeval forests.
Insects and fish-like beings and scaly things with
claws and slime that lived and moved momentarily
appeared and were dissolved and replaced by vistas of bubbling, boiling lava and liquid flame. And
all was fire.

'And then there was only the silence of the
stars, and space, and blackness, and a void which
was and is, and is to come, for in the end is also
the beginning, and this void, being Nothing, could
be created, and this void, being Nothing, could not
be destroyed, and this void, being Nothing, is and
was and will be, and this void, being nothing, is
not, was not and will not be. It exists and does not
exist forever, has existed and has not existed forever,

will exist and will not exist forever; no words can describe that Nothing which I perceived, and yet did not perceive.

'We are separate from that Nothing, and we judge Time as a series of events. Were we One with that Nothing, there could be no Time.

'And as I gazed, I knew what I would be seeing within the stone, and as I realised that I knew what I would be seeing, I was seeing it. For I was within the stone watching me; and I was without the stone watching me; and I, and the ''I'' that was more I than everything I call ''I'' regarded one another; and as I grasped that I was both, I knew also that the two ''I's'' were One, and they united in me.

'I must have slept. I awoke twelve hours after first looking at the stone. I have not looked at it since. There is within me too strong a desire to cling to my sanity. I do not know why. Sanity does not seem capable of coming to grips with space, time, existence or identity. It provides no explanation. At least I have the consolation that even the insane must know that all these things lie beyond any explanation of them.'

'An incredible tale,' mused Renshawe as he returned the manuscript. 'This Septimus Keen is obviously a very clever man. I wonder, though, if he is anything more . . .'

'That observation, my dear sir, is disappointingly tepid,' replied Mr Sedgemoor. 'I had hoped that the tale would transport you into a mood of enraptured enthusiasm, for if it has not had that effect, your view of literature must be radically mistaken. It disturbs me, Mr Renshawe, that your reaction resembles that of a newspaper critic. You will agree, I am sure, that newspaper critics are men whose gross inefficiency, blundering stupidity, crass ineptitude, oafish bungling and utter incompetence have rightly caused them to be despised by all who possess the smallest knowledge of aesthetics. Forgive my seeming rudeness, for I trust I may be permitted to feel strongly about a matter which has placed me in such dire peril. I remain grateful to you, and will follow your capital advice and turn to Her Majesty's police force. When all these matters are behind me, perhaps we shall continue with our deliberations concerning literature, which ultimately involve an analysis of the nature of life itself. A gentleman with whom I was briefly acquainted was once good enough to tell me that I had brought the most acute scrutiny to bear upon these perplexed and doubtful questions. But I fear that this digression has outstayed its welcome, and I am intruding upon your generous hospitality, besides which I see that it is getting on for six o'clock.' Mr Sedgemoor rose and put on his high silk hat. 'May I express the hope that we shall meet again before the year is out? A thousand thanks, Mr Renshawe, and a very good evening to you.'

The strange visitor bowed himself out of the room. For a long time afterwards, Renshawe sat smoking in silence, contemplating the vacant chair with a mixture of suspicion and bewilderment.

4

The Unfortunate Young Lady
of the Savoy

(The Spaces In Between)

One of the more innocuous and consistent pleasures of Lady Clarissa Mountford was the taking of afternoon tea by herself at the Savoy Hotel each Thursday. The causes of this habit included the colourful assemblage of persons who were usually upon display, the delicately scented flavour of Lapsang Souchong tea, the unimpeachable delights of thin cucumber sandwiches and thickly buttered toasted teacake, and the velvety seduction of fresh chocolate eclairs. This particular afternoon, however, did not seem to hold much promise of diverting entertainment, for there was only one occupant of the splendid hall, a young woman in black wearing an ostrich-plumed hat, whose face was hidden by a veil, and who had not moved since Clarissa had entered.

Clarissa nibbled at a cucumber sandwich. She was not in the best of spirits, for she disliked inexplicable mysteries, and her mind could not resist probing for a connection between a chain of incidents which made very little sense. It was fifteen days since Renshawe had first mentioned the young lady of the flaming red hair, since when she had seen him four times. They had passed many hours in discussing both Mr Potter and Harold Sedgemoor, without profiting greatly thereby, and these gentlemen and the young lady with whose sinister designs they seemed in their separate ways acquainted, seemed as elusive and intangible as an early morning mist upon the moors.

She was distracted from this train of thought by a loud muffled sob from the lady in black, who appeared to be possessed by the most abject misery. Hoping for a release from the tedium which the afternoon threatened, Clarissa promptly extracted a small white card from her handbag, wrote a few sentences upon it, placed it in one of her little white envelopes, and quietly commanded the waiter to bring it to the attention of the unfortunate woman.

Moments later, the lady in black looked at Clarissa, then rose to sit down opposite her, lifting her veil to reveal a face that was quaint and piquant rather than beautiful. Beneath black curls and a high forehead was a pair of hazel eyes that shone as though she had just been crying.

'Thank you so much, Madam, for condescending to notice my unhappy state,' she began timidly. 'I had entirely forgotten that there still exist those whose hearts are kind and whose souls are charitable.'

'It is certainly most distressing to witness such unhappiness in so young a lady,' Clarissa replied gently. 'Pardon my curiosity, for I wondered if I could be of any assistance.'

'I am most appreciative of your concern,' said the young woman. 'My loneliness and misery overcame me just now. It was almost too much for me to bear.'

'You are a stranger to this city?'

'I know it only from occasional shopping expeditions, Madam, for most of my life has been passed in the pleasant town of Brighton. I would that I had never been forced to set eyes upon this repository of shameless sin that is the capital of our Empire.'

'Take a little tea with me,' suggested Clarissa, 'and in the event of your desiring to unburden yourself of the grief with which I see you are afflicted, I can promise you a most sympathetic ear.'

'Madam, you are most noble. Yet I fear that my sad narrative would only exhaust your patience.'

'Come now,' cooed Clarissa, 'I would love nothing more than to hear your tale, and to assist you in any way I can, provided that you are not embarrassed by my being a total stranger.'

'Alas, Madam, my story is such that only a stranger could hear it without my suffering the deepest shame. May I rely upon your complete discretion?'

'You have my solemn word.'

'Then perhaps it is best that I should at last

unburden myself of my appalling experiences. My name is Mrs Arabella Wesley, and I am the youngest daughter of Mr and Mrs Randolph Crashaw, devoted parents whose exemplary standards of conduct are equalled only by their piety, and by the respect in which they are held by all who have the privilege to be acquainted with them. My Papa is engaged in trade, and although this denies him entrance to the highest circles of society, he is consoled by the knowledge that his reputation for honest transactions is without blemish, and that his habits of industry and thrift have made him a man of property. I have four sisters and three brothers, and I can assure you that we were all brought up with the utmost strictness. The slightest deviation from high and dutiful standards of behaviour was visited with a sound birching until we reached the age of majority, and it is my unabashed conviction that the just punishment of our transgressions has rendered us fit to take our places in society with all due decorum. My sisters and myself are in consequence eminently respectable ladies whose accomplishments include the painting of water-colours, the playing of the piano, the arranging of flowers and the practice of needlework.

'Eighteen months ago, at the tender age of twenty-two, I was introduced to a gentleman. His name was Richard Wesley, and he delighted me with the dignity of his bearing, the neatness of his dress, the punctiliousness of his manners, the seriousness of his conversation, and the general gravity of his conduct.'

'He sounds a most remarkable individual,' commented Clarissa.

'He was indeed, as you will see. His occupation was that of a respectable man of business like my dear Papa, and his manner of conducting it was renowed for its utmost probity. He was fifteen years my senior, and I was greatly honoured by his attentions. There is no need to elucidate the details of the courtship which ensued. I would stress, however, that there was never at any time the slightest hint of impropriety, and that a chaperone was always present. He proposed marriage, and Papa gave his glad consent. Six months ago, I stood outside our little church, wedded in holy matrimony to a gentleman of unblemished repute, and I fancied myself to be the happiest woman in the whole world!'

'Yes,' sighed Clarissa, 'that is a not uncommon experience, succeeded though it sometimes is by the bitterness of disillusionment.'

'Alas, Madam, you have given voice to my own sentiments,' said Mrs Wesley. 'I had been given to understand that there are obligations in marriage which decent women bear in silence and never speak of, but this left me wholly unprepared for what transpired upon my wedding-night. I had envisaged that the performance of my marital duty would be succeeded by romantic bliss. Instead, I

was forced, and forced most brutally, to partici-
pate in acts so beastly that I shall blush all my life
at the vile memory. And all this in a hotel bedroom in Boulogne Sur La Mer!'

'That must have been especially hard to bear,
Mrs Wesley. I am surprised that you survived the
ordeal.'

'Only my sense of duty kept me from self-
murder, Madam. I endured all, as martyrs once
endured the thumbscrew and the stake, wishing
only that the earth would open and swallow my
defilement. That all these years of my parents'
stern and loving education should be so disgrace-
fully besmirched . . .' Mrs Wesley broke into a
renewed fit of sobbing, ' . . . and by the husband
whose high-mindedness I had so respected . . . I
doubt if pathos can go further, but it did, and I
do not know if I can bear to tell you what
followed . . .''

'Surely nothing occurred that was worse than
what you have described?' put in Clarissa.

'Ah, Madam, life had further cruelties to inflict
upon my innocent and unsuspecting person. I returned to the matrimonial home with all the self-
respect of a soiled glove, numb with the realisation
that I was wedded to a debauched and unrepentant
reprobate, who hid his filthy passions beneath the
outward semblance of a respectable and respected
gentleman. I counted myself fortunate that he was
so often away on business, or so he said, and I

THE DEVIL'S MAZE

even contemplated flight, but who would shelter a wife who had deserted her husband, and who would believe my shameful narrative?

'As if this was not a sufficiently abominable fate, I one day chanced upon some letters which Mr Wesley had carelessly deposited upon the hall table, and to my inexpressible grief, I learned that even during our courtship, and now despite the bonds of matrimony, my husband consorted with another woman!'

'Dear me,' said Clarissa, 'I cannot fathom why on earth he should choose to do something so lacking in the standards of moral conduct which our society demands.'

'Once more you correctly anticipate my thoughts, Madam. But worse was yet to come. Incredible though it sounds, he proposed to divorce me in his letter to the abhorent adulteress, so as to leave him free to marry her. My eyes swam with tears, and I could barely believe the evidence they presented to me. Oh, why does the Law not allow a wife to divorce her husband?'

'Surely you had done nothing which would be frowned upon in a court of Law, Mrs Wesley?'

'Most definitely not, Madam, and Heaven forbid the possibility! But the monster I had married proposed in his letter to "arrange" matters, and said that he would pay a servant handsomely for perjuring himself as the cited corespondent—a servant! I read what he had written, and I trembled, and as I trembled, my husband entered the room, threw me to the floor, seized the letter, and abused me with oaths which overwhelmed me in their horrible impurity. Dazed by shock and anguish, I made some feeble attempt to plead with him, but he laughed contemptuously, turned on his heel, and strode from the house.

'Consider, Madam, the prospect with which I was now faced. If the diabolical plan succeeded, and a perjured witness was believed, I would be branded as a brazen adulteress . . . who had taken a servant to satiate her loathsome lusts. My parents would disown me, I would be ostracised by all decent human beings, and I would have to bear disgrace, ostracism and penury, until, an outcast from society, I might crawl into domestic service there to drag out a wretched and miserable existence, branded by shame until a welcome death put an end to my worthless life which had once held so much promise.

'One ray of hope lightened my abject misery. The adultress might be cruel and vicious, but at least she was of the gentler sex, and I prayed I might elicit from her some morsels of pity. Recalling her address, which I had seen at the head of my husband's contemptible letter, I wrote to her an impassioned plea, abandoning forever what little honour I had left. I said that I would endure all manner of neglect from my husband without the slightest complaint, and that I would never refer to his liaison if only she would persuade him to relent in the matter of the proposed divorce. To my relief, the woman sent me a civil reply, informing me that she had no desire to precipitate my total ruin. She insisted however, that there were certain matters which could only be discussed in person if all was to be settled to our mutual satisfaction, and requested that I meet her here today, Thursday, at half-past three. The creature even knew that Mr Wesley is at present away upon business!

'I had no choice but to accede to her request, and so, bereft of all dignity and happiness, but hoping to salvage my future reputation, I journeyed to London today by rail. The woman kept me waiting for thirty minutes before she condescended to appear, where upon she drove from me any last beliefs I might entertain concerning the decency of the human race.

' "I have very little to say to you," she began, and my heart sank. "My only adivce is that you do as you are bid. Your husband only married you because you are possessed of wealth which he can use, and the sight of you is wholly repugnant to him. He has always loved me. But that as it may, I was sufficiently impressed by your plea to consider persuading your husband to abandon his ingenious scheme, but only on certain conditions. Obey me if you do not want your marriage to terminate in your utter disgrace. I will come to live with you, and you will tell your friends and family that

I am a servant whom you have employed. In fact, I will become the mistress of the household, and you will be my secretary and maid. I gather that your parents have been strict with you. That is as it should be, for I believe in the chastisement of idle servants, and I counsel you to do nothing that might incur my displeasure. You have twenty-four hours to contemplate the choice between the opprobrium of a divorce, or service to a lady. If you choose the latter, as you will if you are at all sensible, you will signify the same to me by the completion of your first task, which is to make three fair copies of the manuscript I have here.'' She tossed it to me with a contemptuous gesture. ''I am involved in publishing and I require cheap labour. Think upon what I have said, and ponder the alternative. That is all. Goodbye, Mrs Wesley.''

'And with these cruel and unspeakably heartless words, she swept out of this room, leaving me the helpless and humiliated prey of her triumphant evil. And on top of all that, I suspect that I am with chidd! Is it surprising that my self-control proves insufficient?' And the unfortunate lady broke down into another fit of sobbing.

'Mrs Wesley, you are perhaps the unluckiest person it has ever been my privilege to meet. This is all uniquely frightful! Can nothing be done? Can you not inform your parents and implore their assistance?'

'Alas, they are too righteous for the rotten age

in which we live, and simply would not believe such things to be possible. They would think me mad, or else a liar. I am alone, utterly alone!'

'The adulteress sounds utterly venomous,' Clarissa declared indignantly. 'Who is she? Where does she reside?'

'Oh, Madam, I thank you for your concern, but it is quite hopeless. I omitted to tell you that she lives at a variety of hotels under a variety of aliases, so as to elude all possibility of the vengeance of outraged wives. But perhaps you saw her leaving as you entered this hotel? She is fashionably dressed, is of pretty, if haughty appearance, and is distinguished by tresses of flaming red hair.'

'Oh . . .' said Clarissa very slowly.

'Madam, I seem to have upset you in some way . . .'

'No, not at all, Mrs Wesley. I am still stupefied by her odious behaviour. You said just now that she claimed to be involved in publishing. I confess I am curious as to the nature of the manuscript which she gave you. It might supply some clue regarding her true identity.'

'You may read it if you so wish, Madam, but I hope you will not censure me for having it on my person. It is a most indelicate tale by a certain Mr Septimus Keen, is wholly unfit for the eyes of the young, and sorely requires either the judicious editing of the late lamented Dr Bowdler, or else what the poets would call ''the purging fire''.'

'I quite understand, Mrs Wesley.' Clarissa took the proffered manuscript, opened it out, and began to read:

THE SPACES IN BETWEEN

'Demons whispered to me in my dreams the night before I met her. There were cities of incalculable antiquity, buildings of spheres, pyramids and giant flat planes which dwarfed inhuman inhabitants, and soared ever upwards into a violet sky; dying suns and distant stars, holes in space in which other universes lay concealed, and spaces in between the stars wherein monstrous beings shambled, slumbered and endured. I felt not that I was dreaming, but rather that I was being dreamed, and that somewhere in eternity slept the author of my dream. In the morning, the awakening was bitter.

'At times I do not know which life is my real life, if indeed there be such a thing. Dusty brown volumes repose upon my shelves, filled with the histories of my dreaming life, which to me is more life than everything we flatter by that name. When I awake, I am reminded that I am a man living in a city that is now called London, but I see only a city of the walking dead, whose eyes stare sightlessly before them, and who perform meaningless and repetitive tasks in order that their corpses may continue to be animated. Perhaps I once committed some crime, some hideous blasphemy, on account of which I was sentenced to a term in Earth's prison, there to suffer an incarceration of three score years and ten, and from which each night I am paroled. I am reminded of the Chinese philosopher, Chang Tzu, who dreamed that he was a butterfly, then asked if he was indeed Chang Tzu who had dreamed of a butterfly, or a butterfly now dreaming of being Chang Tzu.

'If you met me, you would think me an eccentric hermit who dozes over his books and senseless jottings in a bed-sitting room on the borders of Little Venice. Once there were the houses of the well-to-do, and now sour-faced landladies let furnished rooms to the obscure and impoverished. I am sustained by a small income derived from my facility for sketching, which provides me with a diet of bread, cheese, tea, tobacco and ale. I also paint garish pastels and translucent oils which give substance to my inner life, but these are hardly suitable adornments for suburban drawing rooms.

'I am alone. I have no kinship with the human race save that which is vouchsafed me by aliens like myself, who symbolise their experiences with strange musical notations and harmonies, with bizarre colours and forms on canvases, with haunting words upon a printed page. I do not know when or where my journey will end, but last night gave me intimations of its nature.

'Hitherto I had believed that a vast gulf, an ultimate abyss, yawns between dreaming and waking. I thought that in the world of men, all was ordinary. Yet the meeting with the woman that was pursuant to my dream does something to persuade me that all is not aright upon this Earth, that there are others like myself concealed among you, that at certain instants, the veil is rent to reveal an eternity of chaos.

'Let me try to set it all down as clearly as I can. On the evening after the dream, I was walking beneath the trees of Sutherland Avenue, meditating on the manner in which each house differed from the one next to it, as though each dwelling-place imbibed the personalities of its successive inhabitants. As is my habit, I paid no attention to passers-by up until that moment when I saw the woman, and she saw me.

'She was walking swiftly towards me, a young and beautiful woman with dark hair and full lips. It was not that which caught my attention; I have little interest in such things. It was her eyes. Turquoise in colour, they blazed with an infernal iridescence, as if they were searchlights illuminated by a roaring gas flame within. I noticed then that the woman's nose was slightly beaked, like a hawk, and it was as if she searched for her prey. When her eyes encountered mine, I felt that they were stripping my very being from me, searching for my soul, feeling its pulse in order to determine whether or not it was her quarry. I cannot say if her face was that of an angel, or that of a fiend:

behind it there lurked something remote and inhuman, something that lay far beyond either the demons or the angels.

'Thus I felt her invisible touch upon me: it was a pain, and it was an ecstasy, it was the song of a nightingale in the grip of a snake. I do not recall how we began to talk, what I said to her, what she said to me. We conversed in a language which I knew, though no one had ever taught it to me, so that when she said that dusk was upon us, I understood something of far greater import, though in a thousand years I could not express it.

"I remember her saying that she lived in a house not far from where we were, and that I must come with her. I assented gladly, for in the lilt of her speech I sensed the constraint of some divine messenger. She led me to a stuccoed terraced house, white with a black door, which may have been in Warrington Crescent; I have no memory for immaterial details. We ascended the stairs for what seemed like hours, and it became very cold. I was troubled also by a brightness, even though the sun had nearly set. We entered an attic room, hung with sigils and pictures that were dreams and doorways into dreams, and we sat upon sponge mats.

'I think she told me a story then, though she may have sung me a song, the notes and words of which danced in the spaces in between the stars. There was a refrain to the song, a refrain which vibrated within the walls of the room, then cried out to the stars themselves, and which was the chorus of some unknown and dreaded return. It was in no language that was human, and the notes were of a long-forgotten harmony.

'Her song was a narrative, an odyssey of wandering within galaxies by a race of beings whose heritage had been taken from them, yet who lurked at the borderlands of time in the spaces in between the stars, ever eager to regain the rule that had once been theirs. She sang too of the planet Earth, and how there raged about it a bitter battle between the New Gods and the Timeless Ones of Old. She sang of the spells that would summon the creatures of the Deeps, of the men who had worked these spells, of the hoary volumes in which they hid them.

'And then her song turned to particular events, to an abhorred Book entitled in English, *The Freeing of the Denizens of the Deeps*. She sang of how it had first been scribbled down by a baleful, slit-eyed sorcerer on the freezing desert plains of old Mongolia, how it had fallen into the hands of the fabled Accursed Rabbi of Prague, Rabbi Jacob Simeon David ben Mordecai, how it had been translated into English by Geoffrey Yclept The Clerk, the mad scholar of Oxenford, how the Inquisition had burned all but one copy, which had been acquired by a Restoration rake and antiquarian of evil repute, Jasper Herrick. The forbidden incantations within this worm-eaten volume had the power to rend and tear the fabric out of which our existence in space and time is fashioned, and admit again to our world those Ones who reigned before the New Gods came, those which were whispered of in antiquity as Chaos, Babalon, Uranos, Chronos and Nodens, but these names are but a blind.

'The woman told now of her eternal search for the forbidden work, which had been lost after the hanging of Jasper Herrick, and how this search involved fishing within the very pockets of time itself. Now I was here, I was to help, I would aid her in delving into the depths wherein she sought her prize. I did not protest; I was enchanted; I think I must have functioned as if directed by another source. She blessed me and she cursed me with the knowledge of the wine of the Witches' Sabbath, and my throat felt dry, and I begged and gasped for my thirst to be slaked. I have a dim memory of her rubbing the unguent into my bare skin, and I drained to the dregs the vile and bitter liquid abominations within the silver chalice, and then my spirit was freed even as she sang, and I soared into the beckoning blackness.

'That person who is known upon Earth by my name disintegrated utterly. I had no memories, thoughts, feelings, instincts or perceptions. I was, just as I am, and just as I ever shall be. There was no right, no wrong, no up, no down, no breadth, no width, no fast, no slow, no sight, no sound, no smell, no taste, no touch. And then, though I do not know when, at the center of infinite nothing, I saw a point of light, which grew larger, which enveloped me within its blaze, which flung me forth upon the pylons of space and time, and directed by some remote source that was not my own, I sped like a comet through the fine glowing mesh that was the netting of these pylons, and felt both a helpless terror and a pain that started from deeper within me than any I had ever experienced.

'There was a chaos of undifferentiated sensation. Thoughts and feelings accrued with bewildering speed, then I saw pictures which I recognised like long-forgotten memories. I felt that I had a body once more; it seemed that I knew who I was.

'I was a gentleman of mid eighteenth-century England, whose name I recalled like that of a childhood friend. I was that man in his totality, and I lived in his secure and ordered world. I do not recollect overmuch of my life. I think I was troubled considerably by dreams which controverted all established fact. This did not fit with my position as a member of the landed gentry, though my ancestors were spoken of in hushed whispers by the folk who laboured on the grounds of my estate. Maybe my dreams influenced my tastes without my knowing it, for I recall that they were exotic. I was a bibliophile who had completed the Grand Tour, and whose society was sought by Clubs like the Dilettanti, and the Friars of St Francis of Wycombe.

'Well do I recollect the rites and ceremonies of this the emperor of Hell-Fire Clubs. I witnessed the obscene devotion of Sir Francis Dashwood to the naked figurine of Astarte; I stared into the viper's eyes of the corrupt and dissipated Earl of Sandwich; with the poet Charles Churchill I bellowed barbarous incantations to Satan; I accompanied George Selwyn to the public executions over which he gloated, and to graveyards where cold corpses satiated his secret lusts; and eagerly I joined in the ancient rites and ceremonies of the Unholy Twelve.

'Yet all the while I caroused and whored and gambled, I was aware that something in my dreams, or possibly in between my dreams, was prompting me to search for something of which I knew not the exact meaning. It was a book of some kind, which contained secrets far beyond those in the worn grimoires that whispered spells from their shelves.

'As I recall it, I persuaded Sir Francis Dashwood to have me to stay, and then proceeded to abuse his hospitality by entering his private library one afternoon, though it was clear that all strangers were forbidden to browse within its dusty confines. I hunted feverishly for the Book; I felt sure I would know it if I saw the Book that had appeared to me in my dreams. And then I remember how my heart began to thud within my ribs when I saw something familiar which lay between Dee's *Book of the Concourse of the Forces* and the *De Aliorum* of Junvetius. Instantly I recognised the faded gold letters which adorned the worn black binding. I pulled the Book from its place, dreading the opening of it lest the letters within blast my being. I did not even know why I acted as I did.

'I think I must have heard a footstep behind me then, for I can remember turning round and seeing to my horror a whirlwind of malefic anger in the eyes of Sir Francis's steward, Paul Whitehead. I saw the sun's blinding reflection through the stained-glass windows upon the polished blade of his dagger. There was a sharp, agonising pain as the blade thrust into my innards and twisted. My last glimpse of life, I suspect, was his fat and murderous face, followed by the boarded floor onto which the blasphemous book had already fallen.

'There was an intense light, an intense sound, a scent of gunpowder mingled with the perfume of roses, succeeded by an unimaginable boundless bliss of which the human orgasm is our only poor parallel. I ascended infinite stairways and starways of light until I came to a dot of utter darkness, which swelled to embrace me, and to embrace the whole. For an unknowable period, I was swallowed up in a womb of darkness, then at last released into a space in which millions upon millions of stars twinkled dementedly.

'A voice was calling, calling me back with the siren sweetness of its song. In a chariot of flame. I flashed down pylons, and raced through gateways, past universes of crystals and arches, until I felt once more that numbing, paralysing pain, which is like a cramped tunnel, way beneath the earth, through which one forever crawls. A crescendo of light and sounds burst upon me as I sped out into corridors of time and mirrors, seeing a thousand beings who were all myself, until I found my body in a bare attic room where a woman was singing.

'I was seated on the spongy floor. I opened my eyes. Seated before me was a hag whose skin seemed in a state of advanced decomposition, as if she had been withered and savaged by the weathering of countless aeons. Only her eyes were those of the woman I had met, and they shone with an ageless, turquoise iridescence. Still she chanted her litany, her hymn, and I understood that I had located the Book for her, and that she must now find another who could trace its subsequent history until such a time that she herself could hold it in her talons. Stars took up her refrain, and I heard wandering and sadness, an infinite wistfulness, and yet a cruel, rapacious hunger.

'Behind her, the attic window looked out onto an eternal night. There were flashes, and sparklings, and hissings, and then a scratching sound, as if some small, clawed things were rubbing their scaly skins against the window.

'I screamed. I leapt to the door, and I ran insanely down staircase after crazy staircase, fancying that all the creeping, flapping things of the Great Deep pursued me, down, down, as if I were descending to the very centre of the Earth. A doorway loomed, and then I was through into the clear evening air of the street.

'I have returned to my solitary life, which, to all outward appearances, is ordinary enough. Once or twice I have looked for the white stuccoed terraced house with the black door which I entered that fateful evening, but I have not found it; nor do I expect to.

'Maybe I am wrong in thinking that the veil between the worlds never parts. Only today I found in the gutter a clay tablet the hieroglyphics of which bespoke a Neolithic origin, but the tablet was unquestionably modern: where did it come from? Then there is the Maze in Shropshire, the perfect dance of which invokes who knows what forces, or so it is said by the country folk who dwell within its vicinity.

'It is of no matter. I have found what I have sought. I can return to my dreams. Soon enough I will be dead, and I can once more endeavour to join my cousins at the outer edge of time. Together in the Deeps of Space we will prepare our return to the planet we once ruled. Together in the Deeps of Space we will celebrate the rites of the powers that will assist our eventual entrance. Once more will I voyage forth to an unknown destination, there to encounter my brothers and sisters in our

quest for the Book, the blasphemous Book, the
Book that heralds our triumphant return to our
rightful home from the spaces in between.'

'What a fearful tale!' exclaimed Clarissa, handing
back the manuscript with one hand, and pouring
tea with the other in unaccustomed haste. 'I wonder what type of person is this Mr Septimus Keen.
He is definitely an interesting author, but I suspect
he is not very nice.'

'I would not know, Madam, and I have no
desire to know either,' replied Mrs Wesley. 'But
you have not by any chance encountered the woman
I described?'

'No,' said Clarissa very firmly. 'I have not.'

'You are singularly fortunate. Madam, I thank
you for the extraordinary kindness you have shown
me, and I cannot possibly impose further upon
your good nature. Each one of us must ultimately
learn to bear Life's tribulations with Christian
fortitude, and I, alas, am no exception. Farewell.'

Mrs Wesley replaced her veil, rose, placed some
money upon the table which she had previously
occupied, gathered up her bag, and departed, her
shoulders heaving with sighs and sobs.

Clarissa momentarily entertained the thought of
endeavouring to detain her, but realised this to be
an impossibility. She wished fervently that her tea
might by some alchemy be transmuted into brandy,

for the encounter had disturbed her profoundly. It was not just the queerness of the tale she had just heard. It was also the suspicion that Mrs Wesley's departing sighs and sobs had borne an uncomfortable resemblance to girlish laughter.

5

The Amusements of the Demented Doctor

(Just a Doll)

Dr. Elias Lipsius regarded the burning orange glow of the sky as the sun set over the housetops still glistening from the rain of the afternoon. He was of that breed of men to whom sunset is a sacred time, heralding the coming night like an overture before an opera. Soon the gas lamps would be lit, to flare with garish flames flickering on the faces of the passers-by and bestowing an eerie illumination on the actors in the great drama which moves every great city.

It was difficult to tell how the sight of London at sunset had affected Dr. Lipsius tonight. To all appearances, he was simply a well-dressed gentleman of pleasing countenance who contemplated a moment of the day with quiet enjoyment. After a time, some thought appeared to strike him, and evoked from his thin, moist lips the faintest shadow of a smile. This was succeeded almost immediately by a loud rap upon the door.

Dr. Lipsius gave no obvious sign of noticing the knock, but turned and walked towards his Japanese writing desk, which had been exquisitely carved, crafted and lacquered, He gave no sign of recognition to the butler, who had entered after the knock and who now drew the thick velvet drapes, lit two lamps and served the doctor with a glass of sherry. Dr. Lipsius had trained his servants to work silently and almost invisibly. Only the butler possessed the privilege of announcing his impending entry with the morning knock and the evening knock, which were part of the daily ritual Lipsius had established within the household. His duties discharged, the butler left the room. Dr. Lipsius had not spoken to him and rarely did.

The master of the house sat down at his desk and surveyed one section of his domain with every sign of satisfaction. His study was large and softly lit, and upon the walls there was rich paper, designed by one who had learned from William Morris, though it is doubtful if Morris would have approved. The artist had used many colours in luxuriant profusion to create outlandish orchids, with long stems which writhed and intertwined like a nest of serpents. Other objects in the room reminded Lipsius of his travels: a Buddha of gold from far Indo-China; a dancing Shiva from Madras and a Kali devouring her children from Bengal; the sword of a Japanese samurai, the keen blade of which had severed more than one head: a crudely wrought stone phallus from Siberia: an idol in wood with wide staring eyes from the jungles of blackest Africa; a whip of many thongs from a fakir of Mesopotamia; and many other curious objects of power, including the knife they had given him in Paris decades before. Dr. Lipsius reflected on his original initiation and knew that his mentors then would be delighted with him now. The drama to which he had dedicated his resources had commenced, and he intended a crowning achievement in perverse artistry.

He had just finished his first glass of amontillado, which he normally took for thirty minutes, when an elegantly dressed gentleman entered quietly, seated himself in an arm-chair, lit a Turkish cigarette and, as was his custom, smoked for a time in silence. He too ignored the butler, who entered to serve more amontillado and whose departure went virtually unnoticed.

The yellow, beady eyes of Dr. Lipsius regarded the smooth, smiling, clean-shaven gentleman from beneath their fleshy lids.

'Well, my dear Davies?' he enquired at last.

'Oh, very well, my dear doctor,' Davies responded languidly. 'The drama proceeds as conceived and bestows much gratification upon all sufficiently fortunate to be participants.'

'The climax is not in doubt?'

'You will witness,' Davies smiled, 'a nicely managed crescendo, I assure you.'

'Capital,' said Lipsius.

He had been acquainted with Davies for over five years, time enough to become aware of that gentleman's considerable capabilities. Davies and his two associates had fulfilled some of the finest of the doctor's dreams, yet Lipsius knew all too little about them. His most strenuous efforts to discover more had failed almost entirely, a most unusual circumstance for him. All three personages had adamantly refused to reveal details of all of their past and much of their present. That was a price one paid for their services and Davies had made that clear at the start.

But what manner of man was he? It was difficult for Lipsius to tell. As Davies, he lived the life of a wealthy and well-connected man about town, a polished idler of the pavements. He resided at The Albany, his club was Boodles and he was a frequent guest at the dinners of Lady Dorothy Nevill. He had love affairs with married aristocrats and attractive actresses. His political principles were disdainfully Liberal. There were so many men in London who were very like him. Whenever Davies played a role, he bascially played Davies, so one could learn little more of him from that. To complicate matters, he had the habit of disappearing for periods of the year, when all efforts to trace him proved fruitless. Where did he go and who did he become? It was impossible to know if he was really someone else who *played* at being Davies. Or perhaps the appearance *was* the reality, and wherever he went, he carried on being Davies. It was a perplexing problem.

'I always appreciate your amontillado, doctor,' Davies remarked. 'It never fails to remind me of Poe and *The Cask Of Amontillado*. Now that was an exquisite revenge, executed with the utmost style. I adore revenge,' he murmured dreamily, 'for cruelty is never dull.'

'It can be,' Lipsius returned evenly, 'if it is done without artistry.'

'Then I don't hold it to be cruelty, strictly speaking. It is merely butchery and hence boring.'

'In that connection,' Lipsius said softly, 'I cannot prevent myself from thinking of our friend, Richmond. I find that his brutality is often rather lacking in polish.'

'Yes,' Davies replied as he extinguished his cigarette, 'but it is the necessary foundation stone of my style and of Helen's. Because he is brutal, we can be refined. Besides, I'm really rather fond of a little bracing vulgarity. Occasionally, I visit music halls and derive great profit and enjoyment from popular songs. You see, my dear doctor, the factor of balance is vital in any question of aesthetics, and it is to problems of aesthetics and ethics that I have devoted many years of profound study.'

'More of your ingenious paradoxes?' The doctor raised an eyebrow.

'There is nothing paradoxical about the colour of human blood in the sunlight,' Davies returned easily. 'It is the most astonishingly beautiful colour in nature.'

'My dear Davies, I entirely concur with your sentiments. But how are you to justify the gratification of your sensibility in terms of the ethics you speak of?'

'Simply.' Davies sipped sherry.'I could hold to the position that the ultimate truth about the Universe is that nothing is true and everything is permitted. If you believe that, then ethically, you may do as you please. Or alternatively,' he paused momentarily, 'I could argue that a good man is one who bestows happiness, and there are many who would give their assent to that proposition. Now, consider the results if I murder a man in order to see a beautiful colour. That will make many people happy. The police will be happy because they have a crime to solve. Journalists will be happy because they have something to report. Their readers will be happy because the public loves nothing more than a good, grisly murder. The victim will be happy because, as the Church assures us, he has passed on to a much happier place than this vale of tears in which one may be murdered at any moment. His friends and relatives will be happy if he leaves them money, and if he has none to leave, they will be happy to have a nuisance abated. Nor should we omit my own happiness in contemplating the colour of blood in the sunlight, or that of my associates in hearing

of a deed stylishly performed. You see, my position
is irrefutable. I am really a very good man.'

'How amusing that you wish to perceive yourself as good,' Lipsius commented silkily.

'You misunderstand the difference between us,
my dear doctor. You embrace evil. It is your
reality. To me it is merely an illusion, as good is
an illusion, and so I play with both.' Davies smiled.

'Be careful,' cautioned Lipsius, 'or they may
play with you. I have only just read a story on that
theme.'

Davies glanced sharply at the doctor.

'Septimus Keen?' he queried.

Lipsius nodded and held up a manuscript of
stiff, creamy paper.

'I am most grateful to Septimus Keen,' Davies
commented. 'I have rarely followed so fascinating
a trail.' He rose, took the proffered manuscript,
seated himself once more, lit a cigarette and proceeded to persue:

THE OTHER ONE

'No, I am not responsible for my dreams, I thought
then and insist now. I am what I am and do not see
how I can be blamed. Judge me if you please but I
remain beyond your judgement because I am outside your comprehension and you are not in my
position. I will tell you my tale clearly and calmly.

I doubt if you will understand, and yet you must try. You did say that you were interested.

'It was in a certain Summer that I adopted a particular mode of life, which in many respects was most congenial. For I lived in West London, in a quiet, drowsy and secluded street which was lined with populars and whose gardens displayed the lilac, the laburnum and the blood-red may. I had, to all appearances, no occupation but idleness, though I passed many strenuous hours in the chase of the phrase through the wild woods of writing. During the days when I accepted the blessings of leisure, I explored the tranquil streets, walked by the sluggish river and sipped good ale in secluded taverns. I had few visitors and rarely saw friends, though I often exchanged pleasantries with the keepers of small and respectable shops, which abounded in the district. All around me, there was the gentle, domestic peace of regular lives accompanied by sober and common thoughts. I responded to it and lived temperately.

'It was about a month or two after I had taken this way of living that my tranquillity was troubled by a curious dream. I had given some attention to the study of dreams and fancied I understood a little of this fascinating science. There are dreams which dramatise our worries and preoccupations, often in the form of symbols. There are dreams which express our inner conflicts and ultimate desires to which we forbid the light of day: yet if we had the key, we could unlock our souls and understand our selves. Some hold that there are dreams which foretell the future, and this may be so. There are also dreams which seem silly and senseless: I once pursued the Prince of Wales through a succession of dreary suburbs via omnibus, in order to accompany him to a low-down music hall. However, the dream of which I write baffled me, for it fell into no pattern with which I was familiar, and possessed a disturbing clarity and consistency.

'I dreamed that I was someone else; that I lived his life and possessed his past. He was a man of about my own age, though in other respects, he was a striking contrast. Unlike myself, he had a well-barbered beard and he dressed with a consciousness of rigid respectability. His chambers near Oxford Circus were in a Queen Anne street noted for its elegance, propriety and decorum. The little paid employment he had was owing to a government sinecure obtained through blood, for he was distantly related to Her Majesty the Queen. He was a prosperous gentleman of leisure, yet he gave much of his time to private study of the sciences, cultural enjoyments and philantrophic activities. In all matters, he was a pillar of society and treated with respect by all whom he encountered.

'This, then, was the man I became, and I became him as he returned to his chambers from some labour of charity shortly after night had fallen. I stared into a glass, and I say 'I' for it was no longer 'he', and felt rising within myself an insensate desire coupled with a frenzied excitement over its accomplishment. There was the knowledge that my desire was forbidden, yet this served only to fan the flames of appetite into a devouring blaze. I had to act at last, I knew, and I had to act tonight.

'With an effort, I controlled emotions whose turbulence threatened an explosion of madness and calmly and deliberately set about my preparations. I washed my hands and changed my clothes, donning a black frock coat with white shirt, cravat, and grey trousers and flinging around my coat a cloak of black. Naturally I would take my high silk hat, and my cane, my gloves, my large black bag and within it my instrument of vengeance. The street lamps were lit as I emerged from my dwelling and set off in the direction of Holborn. I walked for a while, enjoying the night air, which was sweet and smokey, and noting the cheerful expressions of other strollers. At Holborn, I took a hansom going east through deserted regions unknown to many, where the streets are dingy, dim and sparsely lit with lamps of cheap oil, and on towards the docks and the dwellers of the slums.

'I alighted from the cab on the perimeter of Whitechapel and walked softly through its lanes and alleyways, breathing in the smells of cheap gin and boiling cabbages. Passers-by, poor, dirty, drunken and unkempt, paid little attention to me, and in any case the streets were dark and my top hat obscured my full features. I ignored the droplets of rain which spattered my cloak and clutching my bag as though I was a doctor, prowled the alleyways with restless excitement in pursuit of my prey.

'At last I saw her, taking money from a sailor by a wall. She was a common trollop of the streets, but her face reminded me of someone and aroused me, and I knew it was she who must be punished. As soon as she was alone, I approached her with smiles and a gold sovereign. Naturally, she was eager for my custom and accompanied me through the crooked streets and twisting alleyways. All the while I watched for passers-by. It was only when we entered a deserted dead end that I let her go on ahead and opened up my bag.

'I shall never forget the astonishment upon her vain and foolish face as I thrust her against the wall, clapped a hand upon her mouth and held up before her eyes the blade of sharpened steel. Then I called her a forbidden name and with all my strength, drove the knife into her midriff and ripped through her belly. I felt the soft flesh yield to the cold, sharp steel and the warmth of her sticky blood upon my hands and experienced ecstasy. All consciousness of self dissolved and there was a rapture of union with some great and awesome force . . .

'. . . and I can write no more of this, for it seems that I passed into another dream, and perhaps there were others, for I awoke some time later.

2.

'It is understandable, then, that the following morning, when I recalled my dream over tea and toast by my window, I felt acutely disturbed. I wondered what could possibly have caused that dream, for I was not conscious of any fantasies in which I murdered women. I tried to dismiss it all as "just a dream" but the memory remained to trouble me. Finally, I resolved upon a walk and passed a pleasant hour in strolling around Turnham Green before deciding on an intellectual debauch with a bad but amusing newspaper.

'It was outside the newsagent's shop that I saw the headline which made me recoil as though I had been struck. Panic shook me and my heart pounded as I bought my paper and stumbled away, my eyes riveted upon the story. Buildings and trees seemed to tremble before me, as though unreal. For here in cold print was the report that a prostitute had been murdered horribly in the East End of London. The murderer had ripped her belly.

'It took some time to get a grip upon myself and think things through clearly. What had transpired? It was, I decided, a case of a dream which foretold the future, albeit a most uncanny example of one. Why should *I* experience it though? And why should I identify with the murderer? I could discern no reason for that. Moreover, *did* the man who ripped women lead the respectable life I had dreamed for him, or was that fantastic invention? You may think me mad, but that afternoon I went to Oxford Circus, found, after some difficulty, the street of which I had dreamed and loitered there for many hours in the hope of seeing the man I had dreamed of being; but I perceived no one remotely like him and returned home disappointed.

'Then, nothing happened for a week or so. The event began to slip in importance as my memory of it receded. It was odd, it was curious, it had mystery and yet like so many events of a similar eerie nature, it led nowhere and proved nothing. I became calm again and proceeded with my peaceful routine. All was going smoothly until the night it happened again.

'In its manner of occurrence, it was practically identical to what had passed before. I dreamed, and once again I was the bearded man of noble birth whose life was, to all outward appearance, impeccable. Once again, it was night when I stared into a mirror and felt rise within me the insensate and delirious passion for vengeance. As before, I dressed with care, took my bag and set off to prowl through the night amidst crime, lust and poverty in search of my victim. For a second time

I found her, ripped her and slew her, as though she was the same woman, bathed my hands in her blood and was suffused by an intense bliss. And this time, when I recalled the dream, it was with terror.

"I had to force myself to leave the house and walk to the newsagent. When I saw the headline outside the shop, I was overcome by a dizziness, by weakness and by nausea. With trembling hands I paid for the paper, which informed me that last night in the East End, the murderer had butchered another victim.

'What was I to think? What could I do? I was seized momentarily by the idea of going to the police and urging them to watch that Queen Anne street near Oxford Circus, but of course they would think me insane, for no court regards a dream as any sort of evidence. Should I perhaps turn amateur detective, await the murderer's appearance, trail him to Whitechapel and arrest him in the act? Yet for all I knew, my dreams corresponded with the facts only insofar as the execution and geography of the murders was concerned. It was possible that the man who ripped women was a middle-aged clerk in Clapham and took the omnibus to Whitechapel.

'For days I was in a restless fever of peturbation and I fear I drank to excess, for I can recall little until the night when I began to understand. That I remember clearly. I belonged to a number of cultural societies at the time and frequently received invitations to attend their functions, which I occasionally accepted. On this particular evening, I had chosen to attend the annual dinner of some society for gentlemen interested in the eighteenth century. My fellow members tended to be respectable, scholarly and sometimes agreeably witty, and I experienced a mild glow of pleasure at the idea of passing an evening in their company.

'Arriving at the club where the occasion was to be held, I entered the appropriate room in a slightly inebriated condition and took several glasses of sherry, accompanied by civilised conversation. I had just neatly capped a quotation of Pope with one from Johnson when a bearded gentleman entered the room, saw me and recoiled in startled astonishment as my body jerked with the shock of seeing him.

'It was the man I had dreamed of being.

'Other members commented on my abrupt agitation, as I excused myself and hurried to approach the bearded man. His alarm seemed as intense as mine, yet we somehow managed to converse within all the niceties of social convention. I remarked that I felt I had seen him before, he replied that he was sure he had met me, we went through a long list of dates, names and places, agreed that we couldn't have met then or there, and commented on how curious it all was. I broached the possibility of discussing our curiosity further and he agreed with an enthusiasm which surprised me. After pointing out that dinner was imminent and we could not talk properly under those circumstances, he invited me to his home afterwards, where, he suggested, we could discuss certain interesting matters in the privacy they required. I assented and we went in to dine separately, which was probably just as well, for the others were regarding us most strangely.

'During dinner, it was almost impossible to curb my impatience. A veil over certain concealed realities was being drawn back slowly: I wanted to rend that veil and perceive the holy mystery. I had suddenly lost all interest in scholarly jest, civilised learning and agreeable wit. After some interminable hours, I was at last able to rise and accompany my strange acquaintance out of the club and to his home.

'We hardly spoke at all on the journey, for at first I could not. He lived near Oxford Circus, in the prim and decorous Queen Anne street of my dream, in chambers exactly as I had envisaged them and around which I stared in a trance of wonder. Then I became frightened of him, though I concealed my fear. It was likely now that he was indeed the man who ripped women and if he guessed that I had divined his secret, he would seek to slay me. Yet when I made some casual remark about the news, and how terrible these murders were, he agreed with me and did not seem troubled in the slightest.

'The occasion warranted hot whisky, for within ten minutes of talking, we were both gaping at one another while our minds spun and reeled at the awesome strangeness of our situation. For not only had I twice dreamed of being him: he had twice dreamed, on those nights, of being me.

'I had much difficulty in grasping that, but it was obviously true. He gave me an outline of my life, my address, my rooms, my habits and my pursuits, and was as utterly astonished as myself to find it accurate. For my own part, I had a truthful picture of his life, apart from the deeds he might dare by dark and which matter I now raised fearfully and tentatively. Had he ever dreamed, I asked, of doing murder?

'My question provoked no visible reaction. He merely thought about it, seemed slightly surprised and then replied that he didn't suppose he had. Throughout the evening, all references to murder, women and blood appeared to puzzle him greatly.

'We talked for a time about our bizarre link and neither one of us could comprehend it. After a few more hot whiskies, we were finding one another most amiable company and it was then that my host made a curious suggestion. What would happen, he queried, if we exchanged lives for tonight?

'"You'd give me your house-key and stay here," he said, "and I'd go to your home and spend the night there. I know it sounds strange and rather mad, but we are in the lap of something quite extraordinary, aren't we? Here, have another whisky.''

'Something in the idea appealed strongly to me and I found myself agreeing enthusiastically to his proposal. We drank each other's health, then he bade me goodnight and departed for my home in West London. There was no need for him to show me where anything was, for I already knew. His chambers were as familiar to me as if they were my own and I strode about them with a strong sense of anticipation.

'That night, I dreamed again that I was the other one. I stalked through black, wet streets in my cloak; wearing my coat; beneath my high hat; the knob of my cane and my bag-handle dangling from my gloved fingers. My senses led me through the grime, wretchedness and dirt to the woman who must be punished and who had appeared again. Then in the alley I drew out my knife, plunged it within her body and ripped her flesh unto death. Once more was I possessed by the ecstasy of the dark force which drove me, and demons drank nourishment from the blood I spilled.

3.

'It was in the morning, when I awoke wondering where or who I was, that I came to understanding and it was through blood. Initially, there was panic, for I couldn't comprehend what I was doing in this set of chambers, then memories of the previous evening came flooding back.

'I rose shakily enough, performed my ablutions, dressed and stumbled around the rooms in an unthinking daze. Suddenly I noticed that the door of a wardrobe had not been shut properly. I went to do so and was abruptly overpowered by the grip of curiosity. I could not resist the temptation to open the door and see what lay within, and when I did, I almost went mad from horror.

'A black cloak was hanging there, there was a box for a high silk hat, also a white shirt, cravat and trousers, a black bag and several pairs of gloves, on some of which blood was liberally encrusted.

'I say I almost went mad, but I managed to save my sanity in the end. For, you see, I realised that I can't be blamed. It isn't me who murders those prostitutes, it's the man who rips women. It's so hard to explain, but you must believe that it's the other one. I can't help it if he uses my body.

'As for the bearded man, he now lives in West London, where I used to have rooms. He says it's much more peaceful there and he was starting to feel dreadfully tired. He no longer attends meetings of the eighteenth century society, though I still do and it's better that way. You can't blame him either for any of this and he remains totally unaware of what's happening. I've decided not to tell him because it might upset him terribly.

'When I've finished writing this, I'll put on his beard and go and be him again for a while. He's not nearly as exciting but he's much better for this body than the other one.'

'Why can't I write like that?' murmured Davies. 'It's what I've been trying to do all my life.'

'Because you have not lived as he has,' Lipsius answered softly as he took back the manuscript. 'Which is as well, for the price of his life is high. Oh, yes,' his tongue flicked out to moisten his thin lips, 'I have interesting plans for our dear Septimus. Very interesting plans indeed.'

II

It was an hour later when Dr. Elias Lipsius received Richmond in the conservatory, which was illuminated only by the pale yellow light of the sickly moon. However, this failed to disguise the fact that the man was badly dressed, as usual, in an ill-fitting frock coat which had the embarrassing bloom of newness. Contrasted with the geraniums, the camelias, the cacti and the Venus fly-traps, Richmond seemed especially awkward, graceless and unable to deport his bulk with the slightest elegance. His massive fist gripped the small crystal sherry glass as if intent upon crushing it and he drank aged amontillado as though it was beer, a sight which never failed to distress Dr. Lipsius. The doctor sometimes wondered why he bothered with Richmond, who was in one sense merely a lout with gentlemanly pretensions. And yet it could not be denied that the man was useful at all times and on some occasions, indispensable.

Dr. Lipsius regarded the charmless face, with its muddy and reptilian eyes set in pale waxy skin, and recalled the Wanted poster an agent of his had discovered in Arizona. The reward had been ten thousand dollars and the crimes were all Murder. Since the days of that poster, Richmond had endeavoured to improve his appearance with a thick ginger moustache, which melted into a pair of bulbous chin-whiskers. Although this arrangement was slightly repulsive, it was also badly done and therefore slightly comic, and so Richmond was now less likely to alarm strangers with his face alone.

There was, Dr. Lipsius supposed, profit to be derived in the study of so unappetising a specimen, for he did regard himself as a keen student of human nature. The element which interested him most about Richmond was that the man seemed in a perpetual state of controlling an inner rage. One sensed that rage in the air around him, one smelled it in his profuse perspiration and it was as though he was surrounded by an aura of deadly menace.

The doctor glanced at the large, strong, muscular hands and noted that Richmond was scratching his fingers, as though he itched to be with someone he could strangle.

The thought crossed Lipsius' mind, as it did from time to time, that perhaps there was hidden potential here and it could be brought out, encouraged and stylised. Then Richmond drained the dregs of his amontillado and a drop dribbled down his chin, deeply disappointing Dr. Lipsius.

'A whisky, my dear Richmond?' he sighed. 'It is clear that you do not appreciate my amontillado this evening.'

'Thank you, doctor, I don't mind if I do,' Richmond returned heartily. 'Sublime amontillado though it is, it would nevertheless be a pleasure to accept and partake of a glass of whisky.'

The butler, who had been standing in attendance by the doorway, proceeded to fulfill the request. Richmond watched the preparation of his whisky with almost indecent impatience, then once again drank it as though it was beer. Dr. Lipsius was tempted to despair of the man were it not for the improbable though not impossible suspicion that Richmond was acting.

Who was Richmond? Dr. Lipsius had frequently pondered that problem but knew little more of him than of Davies. He was Wanted in the West of America, where his crimes had apparently been hideous in nature. Then five years ago, he had appeared in London with Davies and Helen. At present he resided in a large and ugly red-brick villa by Putney Hill, which he had furnished lavishly and in execrable taste. He amused himself with amateur boxing, drinking, eating and visiting popular theatres, the music halls and Mayfair's finest brothels. His political views were resolutely Conservative and invariably uninformed. Whenever he acted in the dramas they performed, Richmond always played men who weren't gentlemen, but who craved gentility without attaining it; like himself. Dr. Lipsius did not entertain a high opinion of Richmond's thespian skills. He had a tendency to overdo matters and he always made errors of detail which marred the conviction of his role. Because Richmond was a bad actor, Lipsius reasoned, he was not playing a role now but was simply being Richmond. Nevertheless, one could not be certain, for he too chose to disappear at certain periods of the year, and vanished for a time without trace.

'My dear Richmond,' the doctor said pleasantly enough, 'tonight I have a little present for you, and I trust that you will learn by it.'

"'A present?' Richmond echoed, cocking his head. 'It is always most deeply gratifying to accept a gift from you, doctor.'

'Do you recall,' Lipsius continued, 'a little task you performed for me some while ago?' The man looked a little baffled. 'Last March, I believe.'

Richmond appeared to ponder the matter, then a light of recognition dawned briefly in his eyes and he chuckled.

'That was the man who had an accident, as I now recall,' he declared cheerfully. 'This accident unfortunately had the dramatic effect of severing his head from his body, and if I remember rightly, an axe was involved.'

'Yes, it had to be done with one stroke,' Lipsius reminded him. 'No untidy hacking or incompetent butchery. You executed the task splendidly, my dear fellow, and your memory of its nature appears eminently satisfactory. There was, however, one other detail, I believe.'

'The head,' said Richmond, after a pause.

'Correct. And you could not understand why I would want it. As I told you at the time, that was entirely my affair, but I have chosen now to disclose a little secret.' The doctor sipped sherry. 'You may be aware that my travels in the East have familiarised me with all manner of human customs and here I have chosen to follow one. I had a man murdered because he betrayed me. I did warn him what his fate would be in that instance, but he very foolishly ignored my advice. However, I have tired of amusing myself with him, and so I would like you to have this as a souvenir.'

The hand of Dr. Lipsius extracted something from the pocket of his smoking-jacket and proffered it to Richmond. The man looked at it and as he realised the nature of the object, uttered a cry and recoiled while the doctor observed his reaction with interest.

'I told him I would hold him in the palm of my hand,' Lipsius murmured as he regarded the shrunken, human head. 'Here. Wear him on your watch-chain. It is a fitting end for him, is it not?'

III

Dr. Elias Lipsius invariably sat down to a candle-lit dinner every evening at one minute past eight precisely. On this particular occasion, he was joined by a girl with a quaint and piquant rather than a beautiful face, whose eyes were of shining hazel, and they enjoyed a repast of oysters, followed by steak tartare, and afterwards in the French style, a portion of buttered spinach.

It was Helen who most exercised the ratiocinative faculties of Lipsius, yet he knew even less of her than he did of Richmond or Davies. It had often crossed his mind that she might in actuality be the sister of the latter, and once they had played brother-and-sister roles with complete conviction, yet the doctor could not be sure. Helen had chosen to live alone, and possessed two small and stylish houses, the one in a fashionable district in London, the other in a Regency crescent of Bath. She visited all the most reputable shops, took tea with hostesses, spent evenings and sometimes nights with wealthy and handsome admirers and, in a departure from this pattern which surprised Lipsius, retired for long and solitary walks by the sea, in the woods or on the hills, appearing to divine a secret ecstasy which lurked in lonely places.

Lipsius had only praise for Helen's acting, which was also distinguished by a certain curious versatility. She liked to play strongly contrasted parts of women in the various roles to which men assign them. She could play a maid or a governess, a street urchin or a demure debutante. She was a most convincing nun, and was equally adept in the role of an adventuress from the demi-monde. Dr. Lipsius was inclined to suspect, therefore, that 'Helen' was another mask this intriguing woman had chosen to adopt. It was impossible to discover where she came from, and it was vain to ask where she went each year at certain times, for no efforts to have her followed had succeeded. At some point between London and Paris, Helen simply vanished, only to reappear suddenly or unexpectedly weeks or months later.

There was a streak of perversity in Helen which appealed strongly to the doctor. It showed, to give instance, in the manner she treated Richmond, which was usually with asperity bordering on contempt. It was clear to Lipsius that Richmond desired Helen, and so resented her behaviour bitterly. Helen was aware of his feelings, did not reciprocate them at all and amused herself by taunting the man, arousing his anger and then forcing him to control it.

'I always find you *such* agreeable company, my dear,' Lipsius said as he patted his lips with a napkin, 'because it is evident how enormously you enjoy our work.' Helen laughed. 'Pardon my intrusion, but which aspect of the work do you enjoy most these days?'

The girl thought for a moment and sipped her wine delicately. When at last she spoke, it was slowly and thoughtfully.

'I think it is the instant when I betray a man who has trusted me.' Suddenly, she giggled. 'I love to see the bewildered pain on their dear little faces.'

'It sounds most amusing,' Lipsius commented approvingly.

'Oh, it is.' Helen recrossed her thighs with a rustling of her petticoats. 'Women are infinitely more ingenious at inflicting pain than men, doctor. You should know that by now. Why, I am reliably informed by persons of authority that in primitive African tribes, the men capture prisoners for the women to torture. The male of the species is often a brute: the female of the species is cunning and deadly.'

'Madame, I have doubts as to the wisdom of your expressed opinion,' Lipsius returned politely but firmly, 'and would counsel a reconsideration of evidence ensued by appropriate reflection. It is the male who excels in the conception and execution of the ultimate in evil, though a female may lead him to it. Why,' he smiled slightly, 'our dear Septimus is also of my persuasion.'

'Our dear Septimus would be,' sighed the girl, and then she laughed. 'It is not inconceivable that I may fall in love with him . . . but no,' she tossed back curls of rich, black hair, 'that would mar the drama and affect its conclusion lamentably.' Helen paused, then noticed something which the doctor was holding and regarded it eagerly. 'You have another manuscript?'

'The morning post brought many delights, but none to excel the package of this evening.' Dr. Lipsius handed a thick pile of small, square sheets of paper to Helen. 'It illustrates my point very neatly at this juncture.'

The girl accepted another glass of Nuits St. Georges and gave all her attention to:

JUST A DOLL

'The thinking of an infant, of a sorcerer, of a madman: it appears to me that these modes of thought are markedly similar, as the ensuing account is intended to demonstrate. If at moments, I write it as a child, it is because I was a child when these events transpired. There are many who will doubt my veracity, or else they will impugn the accuracy of my recall, all because they cannot bear to admit that the truth may be strange. Let them disbelieve me then, for as I shall show, they serve my purposes most admirably.

'When I was aged five, my parents moved to Brighton, where they took a Regency villa near the sea-front. As I later understood, the move was in connection with business interests of some nature and which involved my father and his sister-in-law, who had lived in the town for many years and who, unlike my father, was possessed of great wealth. However, no one explained that to me at the time. In common with most children of my generation and social class, I spent little time with my parents and was initially brought up by a governess. Papa and Mama were remote figures of authority. Generally, I saw my Papa twice a day, at morning and evening prayers. Occasionally he would summon me to his study and question me earnestly about what I was learning. I saw Mama at prayers too, and she used to spend an hour a day in the nursery with me. Occasionally, my parents attended some grand social function, and always before they left the house, they called on me and displayed their evening finery.

'My governess was called Miss Grace. She was a spinster in her thirties who had a sweet face and was not unattractive, though her dress and demeanour were invariably sober. She was always faultlessly polite to my parents. She was also good and kind to me on the whole, and I think I loved her insofar as a small child can love. Although most authorities on the subject considered it essential to be very strict with children, in my case this was really unnecessary as I was eager to please and therefore obedient by nature. Mrs. Grace rarely thought it fit to punish me, although she had full authority to do so.

'I had never received what she told me was the worst punishment that could be inflicted: a birching. She had been known to threaten me with it, which always aroused terror in me, for it seemed too dreadful for words. I understood from her that I would only be birched if I did some deed too dreadful for words. Miss Grace had shown me the birch once when I had been especially naughty, and I had almost fainted from fright. The instrument had been kept since then in a cupboard in the nursery, and I always detested having to open that cupboard when searching for other objects. The sight of the thick instrument with its many cruel twigs was enough to induce a fit of trembling.

'Soon after we settled in Brighton, my mother's sister came to call. Her husband had died some years before, leaving her with a daughter whom my aunt brought to tea, and that is how I met Vanessa. She was one year older than I and extremely striking in appearance. Tall for her age and very slender of build, she had a pale, oval face, a tilted nose, freckles and bright blue eyes, framed by a mane of wavy chestnut hair. She wore a very fetching bonnet and an exquisitely pretty white dress, which fell to her knees in a froth of lace and flounces. With her, she brought her doll, which was dressed in similar fashion. Initially, I wanted to like Vanessa, for I was lonely and wishing for a playmate, but on our very first encounter, I sensed qualities for which I did not care. We exchanged few words, since children in adult company should be seen and not heard, but afterwards when Miss Grace told me I would be seeing much of Vanessa, who was ''such a nice, sweet, pretty girl,'' I experienced unease and anxiety.

'My feelings were to be justified amply by events. For over the ensuing months, I spent much time in the company of Vanessa. We were introduced to one another's nurseries and my Miss Grace met her Miss Mansfield. We were taken on walks and excursions together. Sometimes I went to tea in Vanessa's nursery and sometimes she came to tea in mine. Because we appeared to behave well together, our respective governesses often let us play without their supervision, and it was then that the truth about Vanessa was revealed.

'Not only was the girl older and more mature: she was also bossy, domineering, deceitful, snobbish and spiteful, which no living soul realised except me. In adult company, she became all angelic innocence, childlike sweetness and dutiful obedience, but once alone with me, she delighted in the infliction of pain for its own sake. She was very much aware that her mother was enormously rich and my parents were not, and often commented nastily upon the fact. She was always taunting me and teasing me. Once she told me that my Papa had died, and when I cried because I believed her, she laughed at me. There was a teddy bear I loved and she was always hiding it. Once she hid it in the cupboard where the birch was kept and I cried every night for a week. She also liked pinching me hard and it hurt.

'I had no idea of how I could retaliate. Once I complained to Miss Grace and the words burst from me that I did not like Vanessa. Miss Grace was initially incredulous, for she found the little girl wholly enchanting. Nevertheless, she asked some questions of Miss Mansfield, and Miss Mansfield must have questioned her charge, for in time Miss Grace demanded of me why I was making up untrue tales about Vanessa. It was also impressed upon me that for high and mysterious reasons to do with my father and my aunt, I was at all times to be nice to Vanessa.

'This was becoming increasingly impossible and there was a third factor to exacerbate it. There are a number of conflicting views as to when one first becomes conscious of the influence of sex, and I incline to the position that we are born with sex consciousness. Vanessa's dainty prettiness aroused alarming, violent and ultimately pleasurable sensations within me, which made her cruelties all the more unendurable.

'However, whatever else I may have felt, I was rapidly coming to hate Vanessa with the blackest malevolence. My hatred even extended to the doll which always accompanied her and which she had named "Vanessa." She used to love playing with it, adjusting its clothes, fussing over its hair, cooing over it, talking to it softly and continuously telling it how pretty it was. She wouldn't let me touch it, because she said my hands were much too rough and clumsy and dolls must be handled with girlish delicacy. I still feel loathing when I picture that doll's lifeless and perpetual idiot smile.

'Then came a particular afternoon when Vanessa and I were left to play in the nursery. It was worse that day than it had ever been. Vanessa insulted me, called me unpleasant names, told me I was just a horrid, stupid baby boy and took to pinching me painfully. At first I asked her to stop but she only laughed and pinched me harder. I feared I might lose my self-control and warned her, and she only laughed harder and pinched me more, chanting all the while: "You wouldn't dare, you wouldn't dare, you wouldn't dare, you wouldn't dare . . ." and something exploded within me. I flung her from me, she slipped and fell to the floor, and I leapt upon her, intending I know not what. . . .

'And her fast, excited pants became screams of
outrage as Miss Grace and Miss Mansfield entered
the room.

2.

'The remembrance of what immediately followed
is still most painful to me and I only hope that
those who read me will pardon my perhaps exces-
sive sensitivity in being as brief about it as I can

'For I had at last done the deed too dreadful for
words. Miss Grace thought the crime almost
unpardonable. There was nothing in heaven or on
earth which could justify it or excuse it and there
was only one possible remedy. Ignoring my cries,
she took the birch from out of the cupboard and
flogged me there and then. Afterwards, I had to
make a public apology to a smirking Vanessa. I
have no desire to recall the agony and the hu-
miliation.

'But I remember very well the impotent rage
which gathered in me hours afterwards as I lay
sobbing in my bed and which made me want to
scream and destroy if I was not to burst. In the
morning, I awoke bitterly to a sight which further
enraged me. In the centre of the nursery was something which Vanessa had accidentally left behind,
probably in the excitement of the moment: there,
grinning at me contemptuously, was her lifeless,
idiot doll.

'Something rose in my throat and choked me as there burned within my being an irresistible impulse to destruction. No one was watching as I advanced upon the object I had been forbidden to touch, seized it with trembling fingers and glared into its alien eyes. For some seconds, my fingers fondled the delicate white lace of the doll's frilly dress, then emotion overcame me, and with a strangled cry of: *"I hate you, Vanessa!"* I ripped apart the flouncy fabric to expose the doll's wooden nudity.

'The action seemed to purge me of many feelings and gave me a curious sense of excitement and satisfaction. I held the naked doll within my hands and sneered at it, then ran my fingers up its thighs. I was about to continue with the removal of the dress when noises from other parts of the house reminded me of my situation. Vanessa would be wanting the return of her doll and Miss Grace would be asking me for it. Of course, I could not possibly return the object in the condition to which I had reduced it. This would be regarded as further evidence of my spite, misbehaviour and perversity and no doubt I would once again be punished. I must hide the doll and then seek for a way to rid myself of it.

'I looked about my room. There were a number of cupboards but all were frequently opened by my governess. Suddenly I recalled that the maid who cleaned the nursery only swept beneath the bed about once a month and had performed that action a few days ago. With childish simplicity, I hid the doll beneath it. It must be understood that at that stage, I did not comprehend the significance of the doll Vanessa called ''Vanessa.'' I hated it for what it was, I loathed it because it reminded me of Vanessa, and because it was her possession and she loved it, I was happy to have it in my keep, for in some mysterious way, I felt it gave me power over her. Somehow, I reasoned, it would assist my revenge, though in what manner I had then no idea. What was certain was that my hiding of the doll would cause Vanessa pain and this was enough to begin with. I could afford to dissemble, I decided, and so for the first time, I became an actor, a hypocrite and a liar.

'I was extremely contrite and penitent in the presence of Miss Grace that day, a model of correct behaviour who was thoroughly ashamed of his appalling actions. And when a maid was sent round from Vanessa's house to fetch the doll she had forgotten, I made every endeavour to appear concerned and to be helpful, joining in the search with diligence and some enthusiasm. Under the bed was an obvious place for the searchers to look: because it was so childishly obvious, no one looked there.

'That very afternoon, an event occurred which was to alter my perceptions fundamentally. Although Miss Grace was reluctant to tell me many details of the happening at the time, I later man-

aged to reconstruct the story. After luncheon, Miss
Mansfield took Vanessa for a promenade in the
park. They had been walking there for roughly
half an hour when a man displaying signs of psychological imbalance coupled with inebriation,
emerged abruptly from a copse, thrust the governess aside and assaulted the little girl, ripping her
dress from her body. The cries of Miss Mansfield
were heard by others, who rushed to her assistance
and pursued the assailant, which resulted in his
eventual apprehension. This man, I would add,
was later sentenced to ten strokes of the cat and
some years of imprisonment with hard labour.

'In the aftermath of the assault, Vanessa fainted.
She was revived, only to become the victim of
hysteria, which was succeeded by a high fever.
They put her to bed, gave her nourishment and
seclusion and summoned experts in medicine from
London. All diagnosed shock and prescribed rest
and quiet.

'While Vanessa burned in her fever, I began to
understand what had transpired. To my mind it
was clear that there existed a link between the doll
and Vanessa. In a sense, the doll ''Vanessa'' *was*
Vanessa. I had ripped the dress of the doll: another
had ripped the dress of the girl. I had *caused* the
latter event to occur, therefore, and so whatever I
did to the doll would be done also to Vanessa.

'In a true scientific manner, I put my theory to
the test. First, I gathered evidence by pretending to

change my views of Vanessa and then taking a most earnest interest in her condition. Constantly I questioned Miss Grace for details, and learned that the girl, though occasionally still subject to attacks of delirium, was nevertheless on her way to recovery, though still too weak to receive visitors. My next action was to obtain some pins, and with them I pierced the doll's wood, all the while picturing Vanessa whilst the emotion of hatred churned within me. Soon after, I was told that the girl was suffering from acute stomach pains which baffled the doctors, and I laughed to myself at the confirmation of my theory.

'I did not hurry the execution of my revenge and I revelled secretly in the sad reports of Miss Grace. Vanessa was suffering from an agonising headache; her left leg had pained her and then gone numb; there was some disorder of her liver; there were frequent stitches in the region of her heart; her ears pained her, there was a stabbing in her gums and these were accompanied by frequent nose-bleeds. By this time, the doll was shamefully scratched, spoiled and scarred, for I gave "Vanessa" all the pain she had given me. Once I felt brutal when I recalled my tearful apology to the girl, and snapped the doll's arm: Vanessa must have been lying in a most awkward position, because she fell out of bed and broke her arm, I was told. And I found that if I wound a cloth tightly around the doll's

head, Vanessa had seizures which made it difficult
to breathe.

'Eventually, I tired of my games and feared that
if I continued them too long, the doll would be
discovered. That was when a long, thin pin began
its journey towards Vanessa's heart. Being a child,
I was not very strong then, and it took many days
of effort to push the pin through the wood with my
thumbs. During this time, there was much distress
expressed about Vanessa, whose vitality sank, whose
condition deteriorated, who experienced fits in which
she cried out her pain, and for whom it seemed
that the finest medical attention could do nothing.

'One night, Vanessa apparently experienced a
nightmare in which I was the principal figure. She
told Miss Mansfield that I had appeared in her
bedroom and stalked towards her with a countenance of hideous and twisted malignance, clutching a blood-stained knife which I plunged within
her heart. The memory of the dream made her
hysterical once more, and all efforts to soothe the
little girl proved vain. She continued to rave when
the doctors came to call, and on hearing my name
repeated time and time again, one doctor suggested that I be brought to Vanessa. It was feared
that my presence might harmfully excite the patient,
but the doctor argued that the risk was worth
taking, for my appearance might exorcise Vanessa's
delusion that I was responsible for her sickness.

'And so I was brought to her later that day and

joined her governess in sitting with her in the darkened, hot and stuffy bedroom. Initially Vanessa's face registered alarm, then this was succeeded by a momentary expression of cunning before her features once more became calm. We said little in the presence of the governess. I enquired after Vanessa with sympathy and courtesy and she responded amiably if feebly. At length, Miss Mansfield asked her charge if she wished to be alone with me, and Vanessa smiled and said she did.

'Miss Mansfield left the room. Vanessa reposed upon her pillows. She was very weak and pale, and also beautiful in her way, dressed in white as she was, as though about to meet the angels and take her place among them. After a time, she asked me why I was doing this to her. At first I denied everything but she was dying and she knew. Could I not find it in my heart to forgive her, she pleaded, and her eyes were bright, alert and intent. I told Vanessa that I would forgive her and relent in what I was doing if only she made me a public apology in which she confessed all her crimes and vices. Her blue eyes flashed and a haughty pride came back into her face as she told me that was impossible and that she would rather die. I told her I didn't care then, because she was just a doll. Vanessa began to scream and they took me away.

'That night, no one around her could understand the ravings of the little girl. She shrieked out time and time again that I was killing her, that I had stolen her doll, and that if it was not taken from me, she would die. Those who sat with her could make no sense of it, and shook their heads sadly over her demented sentences: as all the while I pushed the pin deeper into the doll, and at the instant that the pin reached the region of the heart, its head drew blood from my thumb.

'Vanessa had a series of seizures and died shortly after midnight. She is buried in the family vault at the parish Church.

''I managed to bury the doll soon after. It's lying in the earth of the park, near the spot where I think Vanessa was assaulted. I was very pleased with my first murder. It was a perfect crime, for of course no one suspected me and nobody will ever believe my confession.

'Poor Vanessa. She was just a doll after all.'

'Yes,' said Lipsius as Helen finished reading, 'it shows how even in infancy, we can be conscious of the sacraments of evil. Tell me, my dear,' he asked, staring at his companion, 'if you had been Vanessa, what would you have done?'

'Oh, at that age,' Helen returned coolly, 'I would have found some means by which I could take the boy's teddy bear and torture it. There isn't any more Burgundy, is there, doctor?'

6

The Adventure of the
Recognised Conspirator

(Soul Mates)

In the Autumn of 1897, there existed a tavern in Southwark to which the discerning repaired for their refreshment. Subsequently it became an uninteresting public house, but at the time when Charles Renshawe was a frequent visitor, it yet preserved the hospitality of a warmer and more civilised age. Here Ben Jonson had quarrelled with Webster, Samuel Johnson had harangued Boswell, the Earl of Sandwich had discussed the price of virgins with Sir Francis Dashwood, and Charles Dickens had hastily scrawled those miraculous words which would invest his characters with a life more real than life itself.

However, it would be a mistake to suppose that ghosts alone furnished this tavern with its attractions. Many who enjoyed its delights were wholly unaware of their illustrious predecessors. They came for the generous slices of rare beef that were wedged within slabs of freshly baked and buttered cottage loaf; for the punch of brandy and cider, to which the manipulation of the orange and the lemon rinds had added a richly palatable zest; for the unashamed excellence of its fourpenny ale; for the nonchalant bohemianism of its regular patrons.

One such was Charles Renshawe, who, despite his justly acclaimed taste in claret, esteemed plain beer as the emperor of all alcoholic beverages. Few of his acquaintances endorsed his judgement, and fewer still could be persuaded to be seen putting it to the test, and so with the indulgence of his aberrant pleasure, he usually also enjoyed the delights of solitude.

He, however, would have been the first to admit that his initial impulse had been to call not for bitter beer, but for Scotch whisky. Only the fact that it was prior to lunchtime, and hence his rule that the tranquil state of his digestion should not be impaired, dissuaded him from so doing. For he was in a rare state of anxiety.

A man he had known quite well was dead. Before his untimely passing, his body had obviously undergone the most hideous extremes of brutality. The Coroner's verdict had been Murder by Person or Persons Unknown. The murdered man had been a brother within the Order, and Renshawe had perceived the scabrous hand of Dr Lipsius.

This perception was akin to that of an art collector who is correctly convinced that a particular unsigned work is that of an artist for whom he has a passion. The works of Lipsius were principally suffering and murder, and Renshawe's long appren-

ticeship in the detection of the arts of evil had
borne fruit in the instant appreciation of the demented brain of Lipsius in whatever manner of
mayhem it expressed itself. Strands of Lipsius's
web clung to Mr Harold Sedgemoor, and extended
to the unsalubrious personage of Mr Henry Potter,
and to the appalling Mrs Wesley, of whom Clarissa
had told him. As he seated himself by a roaring
fire, he fought against the feeling that he was
holding but a few mere fragments of a thousand
piece jigsaw puzzle.

Renshawe firmly believed that all metaphysical
solutions must erupt from a firm basis in the
physical, and therefore proposed to nourish his
body with ale and the cheddar cheese which he
stoutly maintained should always accompany its
imbibing. He was about to embark upon this welcoming prospect when he was abruptly separated
from it by a hoarse, rasping, and stentorian voice.

'Disgusting!' was the word that halted the cheese
in the midst of its journey to Renshawe's eager
jaws. He looked up, and saw that the word had
issued forth from the mouth of an untidy and
unsavoury individual, who was seated at the table
next to his own, and who had unsuccessfully endeavoured to melt the impression which his visage
assuredly produced upon the unsuspecting, with a
pair of bulbous chin-whiskers. His cheeks struck
one as having weathered many brandies, and his
eyes possessed all the charm of an infant reptile.

Upon the table before him reposed a battered bowler hat; his suit was faded at the elbows, unpressed, and rather too tight for his bulky body; he was smoking coarse shag tobacco in a foul briar pipe; his neck threatened to burst the grimy collar of his shirt; and he was in the process of perusing a sensational newspaper, which was purchased only by the respectable who cultivated a taste for the vicariously salacious. But it was not the unappetising appearance of this gentleman that provoked Renshawe's startled scrutiny, nor even his sudden expostulation. It was the fast growing suspicion that Renshawe had seen him once before, on that fateful evening when he had entered the crowded restaurant and had been witness to the flight of the young lady with flaming red hair, and the hideous visage of her pursuer, who now, he was virtually convinced, sat before him in the tavern, supping what looked like old-and-mild.

Now the man shook his head sadly over his newspaper, and sighed as though all the cares of the world rested upon his muscular shoulders. He did not notice that Renshawe had risen, and moved silently to a chair opposite, until he looked up in the direction of his beer, and their eyes momentarily met.

'A very good morning to you, sir,' said Renshawe calmly. 'I could not help overhearing your exclamation just now, whereupon I looked up and recognised your good self. Is it not warm for the time of year?'

If the man was at all distressed by this unexpected approach, he succeeded in concealing the fact admirably.

'I do not know you, sir,' he replied calmly, 'not even by repute.'

'Then permit me to remedy the situation if I may. My name,' Renshawe spoke easily, 'is Robert Bastin, and I am a private investigator. It would be of considerable assistance to me if you could make your own identity known to me, and then I most strongly urge that you join me in a pint of our incomparable British beer.'

'Very well, if you insist,' he answered, but could not quite hide the flicker of uneasiness that played for one instant upon his features. 'My name is Herbert Tanner, but I am, I confess, at a loss to know what business of yours it could possibly be.'

'That, Mr Tanner, is something which I shall make plain in due course. I can see that you are a gentleman of considerable courtesy, and I thank you for the time you are giving up to what must appear at present to be idle conversation. Let me assure you it is nothing of the kind.' With these words, Renshawe stared meaningfully into the other's questioning eyes, then rose to return, a few moments later, with two foaming pewter tankards. 'Your health, sir,' he proclaimed, raising his vessel, and permitting himself a wolfish grin.

'And yours also,' returned Mr Tanner. 'I doubt, however, if my own will be much improved by this continuing atmosphere of mystery.'

'Ah, my apologies Mr Tanner, for it is my fault entirely, and in all probability due to my deplorable addiction to melodrama. Well then, let us get down to business immediately. I am looking for a young lady. She is tall, of handsome appearance, and is possessed of a magnificent head of flaming red hair. You have not seen her, by any chance?'

'Mr Bastin, I do not know what I find more peculiar,' said Herbert Tanner, 'your sudden accosting of my unsuspecting person, or what you have just related to me. I might indeed be able to assist you, but this I resolutely decline to do until you have advised me of your intentions, and explained to me why you should alight upon myself as a fit subject for your most interesting enquiries.'

'As you wish, Mr Tanner. Some time ago I was contacted by a certain Cabinet Minister, whose name, of course, discretion forbids me to mention. He was desirous of locating the person of his nephew, who has spurned the prospect of a respectable career in favour of the questionable profession of letters. In this path he has been encouraged, it appears, by the young lady I mentioned earlier, who enjoys a variety of aliases and engages in the most dubious activities. My client has told me little more than that, which does not do much towards hastening the successful completion of the case. He does not even know if his nephew is at present in the country, but, he assured me, he had a strong reason to believe that the young lady is in London, and that I must first find her if I am to ascertain the nephew's current above.' Renshawe drank a generous quantity of ale. 'To be candid, I have been rewarded by little that could conceivably be called success. In short, Mr Tanner, I have seen her once, in a crowded restaurant in the Strand through which she passed all too fleetingly, fleeing, as it seemed, in abject terror, from a gentleman of murderous visage who was none other than yourself.'

'Well,' said Mr Tanner, then drained his pint in several voracious gulps, 'well, well, well. This is really the most astonishing coincidence, Mr Bastin. I am now very pleased indeed that chance has brought us together. You are quite correct in your surmise, and I applaud your keen powers of observation. I am indeed the gentleman you saw in the crowded restaurant that night, and, for all I know, my facial expression may well have struck spectators as possessing something of the murderous about it. Allow me, sir, to offer you another pint of this quite excellent beer, and then I shall relate to you my mournful history. You will join me? How very good of you.'

Mr Tanner bustled his way to the bar, while Renshawe watched him closely, admitting to himself that he was somewhat taken aback by the gentleman's frank manner. He ate his cheese thoughtfully, and had just finished his small repast, when his companion returned from the bar.

'I find it remarkable,' said Mr Tanner, 'that you should be a private investigator, for I have many times contemplated the employment of one. My problem is an unusual one, but what you have just told me greatly increases its element of peculiarity. It is all rather like a fanciful novel, Mr Bastin, and I should know, for I am a novelist.'

'A novelist, Mr Tanner? I must admit I would never have suspected so.'

'That, Mr Bastin, is because your idea of a novelist is the product of what you have read in the newspapers, if I may make so bold as to say so. For newspapers give one the entirely erroneous impression that we authors are all devotees of the unclean cult of the sunflower. This is perfectly true, of course, for a very small minority of irresponsible degenerates, but the majority of us are upright, respectable and hard-working citizens, whose productions do much towards raising the moral tone of the society in which we have the good fortune to live. Take my own work, for example. Will you find gilded aesthetes, purple prose, and lascivious ladies? I assure you, sir, you will not. My books, I insist, are manly books, healthy books, wholesome books, which would not raise a blush upon the cheek of a tender maiden, nor a smirk upon the face of a growing and impressionable lad. I write narratives of adventure, in which the moral benefits of discipline and outdoor exertion are continually stressed: *Forty Years Before the Mast*, *In Search of Pirate Treasure*, *With Clive to*

India, and *I Rode with General Custer* are but a few examples of the arduous efforts of my pen.'

'You have obviously enjoyed much travel and adventure, Mr Tanner.'

'On the contrary, Mr Bastin, it remains one of my greatest regrets that I have never set foot outside the shores of our fair island. The exotic settings in which my narratives take place are gleaned from the novels I borrow from Mudie's Circulating Library, which excellent institution, incidentally, is good enough to stock also my own works.'

'Surely, though, your literary success has now provided you with the necessary means to travel?'

'Success?' Mr Tanner raised his large hands helplessly. 'In common with many, sir, you see us novelists enjoying a life of unimpaired luxury. Nothing could be further from the truth. A hundred pounds a year, at fifty pounds a book, that is the reward I receive for my endeavours. A housemaid may perhaps struggle by upon that slender income, but a bachelor desirous of one day wedding a respectable lady cannot. And that is why, I unashamedly admit, I have until recently earned my daily bread, to which my income from fiction is a meagre supplement, as a schoolmaster at Trumper's in Essex.'

'Trumper's in Essex, Mr Tanner? The name is not familiar to me.'

'It is a private educational establishment for the sons of gentlemen, Mr Bastin, and though its reputation may be modest, its contribution to society is quite admirable, for it fits young men to the laudable purpose of governing our great Empire. I flatter myself that as the Master in charge of Latin Unseen Translation and Physical Training, with particular emphasis upon the noble art of Boxing, I am helping to mould the minds of the governing class of tomorrow. A noble task, Mr Bastin, is it not? And indeed, six months ago, I would have expressed to you my great satisfaction with my situation and prospects. My income, though hardly large, was at least eminently respectable, and I had been given to understand that in the not too distant future, I would become Assistant Housemaster of Wellington House. And that, alas, was when the new Matron arrived.' Mr Tanner helped himself liberally to the contents of his tankard before continuing. 'This new Matron, we were given to understand by Mr Trumper, our esteemed Headmaster, was the young widow of a Colonel who had died of malaria in the jungles of Bengal. Her name, we were told, was Veronica Parke. She was the lady you mentioned, the lady with flaming red hair.'

'This is all deeply interesting,' commented Renshawe. 'Pray continue your narrative. I can see that you must be a novelist of well above average ability, for your manner of relating actual events holds me fast within its grip.'

'Thank you sir, for your unexpected compliment,' said Mr Tanner, studying his face closely. 'I shall do my best to justify it, though I wish the matter of my history was possessed of a happier ending. Ah,' he sighed, 'I would that I were not so innocent in matters involving the nature of Woman, for it strikes me, sir, that the deeper one goes, the rottener it gets. This Mrs Parke I speak of has virtually ruined my career. I do not even know why she should venture upon so dastardly an enterprise, but believe me, I owe to her my untimely downfall. Another, Mr Bastin?'

'Indeed, but I shall be the author of our continued refreshment.' Renshawe fetched more beer, and awaited the next episode of Mr Tanner's queer tale with some considerable anticipation.

'Now where was I, Mr Bastin? Ah yes, Mrs Parke. I cannot tell with what competence she performed her duties as Matron. One habit, at any rate, I found singularly odd. She always insisted upon being present at scenes of corporal punishment, deriving from these essential episodes of school life, I suspect, some perverse enjoyment. I personally found her taste unwholesome, and perhaps she was alerted to the nature of my feeling, for she soon resolved upon my destruction. She did not, naturally, do anything that would evoke my suspicions. For a whole term she treated me with nothing but the greatest respect. And then, one day, the impossible occurred. She informed Mr Trumper that she was leaving his employment, and that she could not possibly tell him why. He of course pressed her, whereupon she reluctantly admitted that her abrupt departure was en-

tirely due to the unwelcome advances I had allegedly
been making! She then broke down, and fled from
his study before he could detain her further. I was
immediately summoned and accused. I angrily denied
every word, barely able to believe that any lady
could accuse me of such disrespectful and odious
conduct. I was struck speechless by Mr Trumper's
refusal to believe me, and then I was peremptorily
dismissed from the job which I had performed with
such honour and, I think, credit. I left the school
that very day, as ordered, my reputation in tatters.

'I had just one desire then, that of any honest
man,' Mr Tanner continued, 'and it was to seek out
the vile woman, confront her face to face, and secure
from her an admission in writing that her entire
story was a tissue of lies from beginning to end. And
so, for the last two months, I have scoured London
in search of her, knowing that I would recognise her
immediately. It was a well-nigh impossible task, and
I was sustained in it only by the justice of my cause.
Then one night I caught sight of her in the Strand,
and pursued her into the restaurant in which you
first saw me. Is it surprising, Mr Bastin, that my face
should evince the emotions you saw? For I felt then
that I had lost her, and hopeless rage welled up
within me, and I fear I lost control. I stormed from
the restaurant. Perhaps you saw me do so? And it
was then that I alighted upon a bag which she had
dropped in her flight. The bag bore no initials, and
its only contents consisted of a frightful tale in

manuscript, by a certain Septimus Keen, which says all that needs to be said concerning the depraved sensibility of Mrs Parke.' Here he drew a torn and badly folded pile of paper from his pocket. 'Only my regard for the truth compels me to inflict it upon you.'

Renshawe took the manuscript and thereupon read:

SOUL MATES

'A horror of soul, that is what we shall have. I shall describe a horror of soul. Do not expect from me rivulets of blood and vampires, for I have never yet experienced such vulgarities. Let me describe instead a peculiar kind of horror, a horror so intense and so acute that its merest touch induces in me an ecstasy borne of the union of opposites, a self-love the consummation of which is bliss, the price of which is a life plunged into the chasm that yawns between reality and imagination. Let us then sup at the table of nightmare, a nightmare that shall skip on the claws of reality.

'For a long time now I had prolonged my isolation. It was interrupted only by the chance visits of old friends. I was at work, and at work upon a tale that I thought would exceed even my own anticipations. The work had begun in December and it was now early Spring, for it had taken me longer than was customary, and I was troubled by the nature of the main female character.

'It is perhaps in matters of sex that imagination and reality do most rarely coincide. I did not know whether to pluck a being from my much fermented brain, or to enhance one of the many women I knew with the light of my creation. Neither seemed satisfactory; the women I successfully placed in my tale were all unsuited to its atmosphere. The problem vexed me.

'Many were the solutions I essayed for the purpose of seeking relief. Successfully I induced alcoholic dementia, the careless lucidity of opium, the drowsy mental permutations of hashish, the sporadic intellectual fireworks of ether, none to any great avail. I had momentary mirages of harems, and the abrupt apparitions of unfamiliar phantoms, labyrinths of words, the distances between each one growing ever longer, and contortions of perception, which confused more than they clarified; and of none can I say that they consciously assisted me. Whether they did so unconsciously is quite another matter. The change in the quality of my dreams could have been due as much to a persistent concentration upon the problem as to my equally persistent excesses, both of which long outstayed their initial welcome.

'The fact remains that it was in late March that I first became aware that my dreams possessed an immediate significance. It began with glimpses, glimpses that were grasped with all the fervour that comes with waking early on a chill bright dawn, then forgotten in the stolidity of a hearty breakfast. These slipped through the sieve of my memory until that rainy morning when I retrieved a fast fading image of a woman.

'I christened her Emma.

'In the dreams that followed, I pursued her through doorways that opened onto other doorways through which a thousand Emmas relentlessly passed. Emma was the woman I needed for my tale, for Emma was the woman behind all the women in my tales. My sleeping hours took upon themselves a quest that far outweighed in importance all that I called my waking life, and in dream upon dream I followed her until I feared I might find her at the centre of my very own self.

'As the nights passed, I gradually found myself able to bring down to earth my dream woman. With the aid of my pen, I drew her essence onto paper in my tale. And I discovered as I wrote that there was now no question of Emma becoming accustomed to the atmosphere of my narrative; no, this atmosphere must suit itself to Emma. I began to rewrite feverishly; I thought of nothing else.

'I am trying very hard to be clear at this point, for I do not want there to be any question of misunderstanding. It would be easy to dismiss what followed as a solitary man's mere crazy imaginings, and so it is all the more important that I endeavour to remain detached and clinical.

'For I fell passionately in love with Emma. And as a lover may treat his mistress as his muse, and fashion for her pleasure works of artistry, so did I behave in the matter of my tale. Every skill I possessed was bent to the task of creating a world in which my Emma might see fit to rule. The thing I dreaded most was the moment when my tale would be finished.

'During this time, I found myself comparing Emma with the women I had known, and lamenting the all too obvious fact that my creature of fiction was incomparable. I passed many hours in hopeless daydreams. No longer did I wish, as I had sometimes done in former times, to love an ordinary woman, and by some act of alchemy transmute her soul into a work of art; rather I wished that my love for an extraordinary woman in a work of art might yet perform some alchemy that would transmute her into ordinary life.

'I delayed the ending of my tale, and gave myself up to speculation. Surely, I reasoned, anything that I was capable of imagining would in some place on our planet have its mortal existence? Many times I re-read the Greek tale of Pygmalion, and envied the sculptor who gave life to his masterpiece. I scoured old texts and books of magic for some spell by which I could conjure her to materialise as Emma, not a vision, but rich flesh and blood.

'One night, by the light of my waning and flickering candle, I perceived upon the worn page amidst the hieroglyphs the sigils that I sought. Laboriously did I prepare for my act of magic. I abstained in

matters of food and sleep, and painstakingly drew
and redrew the circles and signs, burnt the perfumes,
wore the jewels. With the aid of mathematical tables
and ancient star-maps that the curious will not find
in any text-book, I calculated the day and hour most
appropriate to the operation. I gathered the herbs; I
brewed the potions; and I proceeded relentlessly
towards the completion of my tale.

'Then came the night for which I had so long and
so arduously prepared. I struck the gong and commenced my curses and constraints, my appeals and
my supplications. From my mouth were flung the
barbarous words, from my hands the signs, from my
feet the dances. At the climax of the rite, I sacrificed
my finished tale, and roared and laughed in ecstasy
as the flames of the brazier licked it up greedily and
consumed it. My attention soared through the clouds
of the symbols I had visualised as I pronounced the
one word "EMMA!" I saw Emma, I heard, smelt,
touched and tasted Emma. I felt Emma, and for one
fraction of an instant, I became Emma. Then I lost
consciousness.

2

'It is said by the Sages that in any magical spell of
desire, the desire, once forgotten in the climax of the
spell, must remain buried if the spell is to succeed.
Therefore when I at length recovered my awareness,
I denied myself the ponderous pleasures of introspec-

tion, preferring instead the calm certainty that my desire would be fulfilled.

'One problem that I would face in the ensuing days dawned almost immediately, however. This was the problem of how I was to fill my time. I had written the tale which I had set out to write, and I had sacrificed it to my desire. What was there left for me to do but wait?

'As it turned out, the hours in which I waited were shortened much beyond my expectations. I slept deeper and longer, up to fourteen hours, and I was troubled by blackouts. These would occur without warning, at any hour of my wakefulness. Soon I no longer knew how many days had gone by.

'I would recover consciousness at any hour of the day or night, and be instantly plunged into confusion. I would not know where I was, or who I was, or what I was doing, or what I had been doing prior to the blackout. Sometimes I emerged from these shadow states with fading memories. They were always of Emma. Sometimes I recalled snatches of my dreams. They were always of Emma.

'Time passed and I endured this state. I suppose other things occurred, but I do not remember them. Somehow I must have found the determination to attend to my personal appearance, for I used to catch sight of myself in mirrors, and be astonished by the fact that, with the exception of my sunken staring eyes, my appearance remained at the peak of vanity. Not to my knowledge did I venture much

from my flat, though I may have done so to purchase
the necessary provisions. Once or twice I discovered
myself in the act of ascending the stairs to the flat
above mine. The discovery was always a shock, and
for a reason which I then did not know, I would feel
guilty and ashamed, and return to my abode in a
state of confusion, convinced that I had transgressed
some unwritten law.

'I began to fight against my growing bewilderment,
a weary, wretched, and restless battle. And all the
while an inner voice urged me to give in that I might
at last find peace. I have a dim recollection of
alighting one day upon a lady's handkerchief, without any idea of what it might be doing in my flat.
Some time later, it vanished. I can give, then, no
clear account of my days and nights.

'I must have left the front door open one afternoon, for that was when an old friend chose to call
upon me, a visit which terminated by haphazard
existence, and brought upon me the full horror of
soul which I spoke of earlier. The sight of his face in
the doorway, garishly distorted by my candlelight—
for my drapes were always drawn—distressed me
unaccountably. Nevertheless I made him welcome
and watched uneasily his bewildered expression as
he regarded the surroundings in which I dwelt. Fortunately he was talkative by nature, since I discovered
I had surprisingly little to say to him. I prompted
him to converse upon trivialities, the weather, social
gossip, political events. Then he turned the conversa-

tion to myself, and observed that he had called upon me a considerable number of times within the last fortnight, but that I had never answered the door. And then, with a sly wink, he requested me to introduce him to the unusually beautiful lady, who, he noted, now lived in the flat above mine.

'I started. I offered brandy, and gulped the contents of my glass before he had even had time to sip. I demanded with a curious vehemence a description, a minute description, of the lady he was so desirous of meeting. He described Emma.

'I screamed aloud. I leapt to my feet and railed at him. I kicked his brandy from his grasp and railed at him with oaths and imprecations. I shrieked; I sobbed; I raged; I drove him from me with curses, never to return. I brushed my hair. I changed my clothes. I perfumed my face. I perspired, I twitched, I stormed out from my abode. I commenced my ascent of the stairway.

'Each step I did recall now as I climbed towards my Emma. I thought of her heavy aroma of musk, her silk dresses, the charms of her soft body. I remembered how many times I had visited her flat, and how on each occasion she had looked more enticing. I dreaded lest another blackout seize me, and bar to me a part of my own being. That is when the pain began to throb in my head once more, when the roaring in my ears began anew, when sigils and signs danced in great Catherine wheels before my aching eyes, when I saw again the smiling face of

Emma, and was smitten by a blinding whiteness as a prologue to the darkness that engulfed me as I slumped upon the landing.

3

'As the waves of nausea and anguished memory receded, I found myself inside the flat, though how I do not quite know. I was in the drawing room, the fussy, familiar drawing room, in which there always lingered that heady smell of expensive scent. Every detail of it was familiar to me.

'I was waiting for Emma.

' "Emma . . ." I whispered.

' "Emma . . ." I breathed.

'I closed my eyes and felt her silken touch upon my skin. I listened to and drank in the rustling of her skirts in the silence.

' "Emma . . ." I cooed, "beautiful Emma . . ."

'I think that when I opened my eyes, I fully expected to see her. When I did, it nigh on drove me mad with the horror of soul I have spoken of, but that came later. For the first objects I perceived were my own clothes, neatly stacked upon a chair. Panic clutched me as I looked down. *What was I doing in a woman's dress?*

'Then I stared ahead into the looking-glass and saw—Emma.'

Renshawe returned the manuscript as a growing sense of unease gnawed at his bowels. He felt as though he was living in a world each inhabitant of which was mad.

'I see you also find the tale obscenely frightful,' said Mr Tanner. 'Mrs Parke, it appears, does not. This is the sort of thing I am up against, you see, Mr Bastin, and I regret I cannot afford to employ what I am sure must be your admirable services. It was very kind of you to tell me more about the sinister Mrs Parke, though I fear it has confirmed my very worst suspicions, and done little towards my correction of flagrant injustice. My only consolation is that I am employing these unpleasant experiences in my new novel, *The Widow of Bengal*, but even here my constant anxiety is forever impeding my choice of words. Well, Mr Bastin,' Herbert Tanner stood up and extended a begrimed hand, 'I must be about my business. Perhaps I have assisted you? I do hope so. It has been a pleasure meeting you, and possibly we may repeat it at some future date. I come here quite regularly these days, and I will be forever grateful if you would condescend to inform me of any success you enjoy, though I am painfully conscious of the fact that I have no right to ask so great a favour.' He shook Renshawe's hand warmly. 'Until such fortunate time as we two again meet,' he declared heartily, and then his broad back receded from view as it entered the street outside.

Charles Renshawe gaped helplessly at the tavern doors. He was no longer sure what he believed, but of one thing he could at least be certain. He walked swiftly to the bar, firmly resolved to analyse the pomposity of Herbert Tanner with the aid of a very large Scotch whisky.

7

The Connoisseur of the Curious and Unusual

(The Devil's Maze)

It was after the chance encounter with the extraordinary Mrs Wesley that life took on a novel and disturbing hue for Lady Clarissa Mountford. Though she did not allow herself to deviate from the rich and regular pattern of her varied social activities, she nevertheless found herself viewing them with a cold detachment which hitherto had not been present. To a small extent, this mood owed something to the behaviour of Charles Renshawe, who had become uncharacteristically morose and withdrawn of late, and in whose company she found herself less frequently. Yet Clarissa knew that she still retained as strong a hold upon his affections as previously, and was led to conclude that the factors which had created his unusual state of mind were precisely those which had affected her own.

Clarissa searched for some means of conveying to herself the nature and quality of her present experience. She compared it to a recurrent nightmare of her childhood, in which she opened a door that led to a familiar social haunt, and was confronted by a sea of unknown and malign faces.

189

But answer came that it was not quite like that at all; that the events she had experienced had about them an elusive quality that she could not grasp hold of. She felt like a blindfolded spectator in a theatre, whose blindfold had been removed so that she could glimpse fragments of the first and second acts, but no more, and was dogged also by the uncomfortable suspicion that her glimpses of melodrama were yet more real than everything which she called by that name. She found herself peering at passers-by in the streets of London, vainly hoping to recognise assistants in lunatic asylums, unfortunate young wives, and ladies with flaming red hair.

It was about five days after her unusual tea that Clarissa found herself in an old curiosity shop that looked out onto a shabby side-street in Bayswater. It was not customary to find her in Bayswater, and that is doubtless why she so often went there whenever she desired to think, for she believed it impossible to think in Knightsbridge or Kensington, where one was always in imminent danger of being recognised. She enjoyed in Bayswater the preservation of a queenly anonymity, and hence could browse at length in half-forgotten shops without fear of unwelcome importunings and attentions from the shopkeepers, which were unavoidable in the establishments which she patronised with greater regularity.

She had been to the old curiosity shop one or

two times previously, but the proprietor, a stout, elderly man with a mane of untidy white hair, followed his habit of leaving potential customers alone. Clarissa was free to muse amidst untidy displays of silver snuff-boxes, flintlock pistols, abandoned eighteenth-century furniture, brass horse-shoes, copper ash trays, iron bed-steads, dilapi-dated volumes of unread print, and haphazard piles of sketches, etchings and engravings. Here and there were carelessly deposited articles which only an eccentric would contemplate purchasing, such as clocks on the face of which wax figurines enacted executions upon the hour, or a set of sixteenth-century golden thumbscrews.

Clarissa had lost herself in contemplation of this assemblage of the lumber of the centuries, and so did not hear the door open and close and the ensuing masculine tread of shoes upon the faded maroon carpet. She remained engrossed in her meditations upon discarded objects, and doubtless would have remained so had the man not spoken after a space of several minutes. In a cultured, evenly modulated tone, he addressed the proprietor.

'Pardon my asking, but I am intrigued by the engraving which I have before me here.' He held up a print, the nature of which Clarissa could not see. 'I believe I am correct in saying that it is the work of Francis Melsomm, and as such, I am astonished to see it reposing here. The last occasion I viewed it, I recall, was when I had the privilege of examining the collection of Dr Lipsius.'

Clarissa could control neither her startled expression, nor the abrupt turn of her head in the direction of the stranger, expensively dressed, smooth, smiling and clean-shaven, and regarding the proprietor with a gently inquisitorial air. The elderly man, however, did not seem in the least bit uncomfortable.

'That may be so, sir,' he replied reflectively, in between puffs at a gnarled briar pipe, 'that may be so, though I do not have the acquaintance of the gentleman you mention. What I do know for certain is that I purchased that print in a job-lot at an auction up Highbury way, and as far as I am concerned, I shall be well satisfied if I receive five bob for it.'

The well-dressed gentleman looked first at the proprietor, and then, very briefly, at Clarissa.

'It is odd,' he declared to no one in particular, 'that items which have been, shall we say "mislaid", are so frequently offered for sale to the general public a very short time afterwards. No,' he held up his hand to ward off the imminent wrath about to erupt from the proprietor, 'I insinuate nothing. My good man, you shall have your five shillings.'

As he handed over the coins, Clarissa found herself torn between the social convention that forbad a lady to accost a gentleman, an an unmanageable curiosity which grew increasingly unruly. Her instinct found voice before her education could suppress it.

'The collection of Dr Lipsius, indeed,' she remarked. 'There are not many, I believe, who are personally acquainted with its contents. Permit me to offer my congratulations to you sir, on a piece of singular good fortune.'

The smiling gentleman bowed briefly to her, slightly elevating the position of his hat-brim with an elegantly gloved hand.

'To accept them, Madam, is most deeply gratifying. It is a pleasure to perceive that so fair a lady has so keen an appreciation of the arts. Some chance and benevolent fate, it seems, has enabled me to make your acquaintance. Allow me to introduce myself. Raymond, Richard Montague Raymond, a gentleman of leisure, at your service, Madam. May I add only that I am a connoisseur of the curious and unusual?'

'Then the pleasure, sir, is entirely mine,' Clarissa answered uneasily, slightly taken aback by the smooth gentleman's polite effusiveness.

'In that case, a celebration is surely most appropriate,' pronounced Mr Montague Raymond. 'For an artistic lady such as yourself may well be able to assist me in the solution to a problem which has hitherto proved most perplexing. May I invite you Madam, at shamefully short notice, to partake of a little refreshment with me nearby?

The establishment I had in mind is renowned both for its wine list and for its unimpeachable discretion.'

Ten minutes later, when they were drinking champagne at a corner table of a small and charming Italian restaurant, Clarissa decided that she had no cause for regret on account of accepting an invitation from a stranger. As he helped her to a second glass, his conversation swiftly departed from the idle lands of flattery.

'You mentioned Dr Lipsius, Madam,' he murmured, introducing the line so skilfully that it did not jar upon what had preceded it. 'You have the pleasure of his acquaintance?'

'Indeed not, Mr Raymond. But I cannot truthfully say that I regret the fact. I gather that his reputation is somewhat questionable.'

'Dear me,' replied Mr Raymond, raising his eyebrows, 'how very extraordinary. And how deeply regrettable. I was possessed of the idea that the good Doctor was of unblemished repute. It pains me, Madam, that we two should move in such very different circles. Why,' his expression became one of supercilious indignation, 'this is the very gentleman whom at present I am assisting.'

'A connoisseur of the curious and unusual,' Clarissa responded archly, 'was that not how you described yourself, Mr Raymond?'

'Quite so, quite so, but one must in all things hold fast to a sense of ethics, the foremost of which is a comprehension of the meaning of personal honour. You add, Madam, to the burden of my predicament. Allow me to explain. A year ago I was introduced to Dr. Lipsius, who since that time has impressed me as a gentleman of considerable charm and weighty integrity, and who is unquestionably a courageous and magnanimous patron of the arts. He is in possession of a remarkable collection, which indeed is virtually a museum, and this collection contains items which were and are of absorbing interest to me. Among them are the works of Francis Melsomm, a young artist who does not deserve the shameful obscurity in which his name at present time resides. Lipsius nourished my interest with his many choice items. He has shown me works of art which few mortal eyes have looked upon, neglected by the dull age in which we live to our detriment, and which one day will receive their rightful dues of worship. And so it is all the more frightful when items from his collection are stolen, to reappear before the profane eyes of the public, priced at five shillings, on common view, in a depressing shop, in a dingy side-street, in the dismal district of Bayswater.'

'How truly dreadful,' Clarissa agreed. 'And would I be correct in my surmise that you have agreed to assist Dr Lipsius in apprehending the thief and recovering his property?'

'Precisely, Madam, precisely. A thankless task in many ways, yet I remain convinced that its accomplishment is essential to my continued ease.

A few more days such as ths one, and I shall have restored the collection. The thief, alas, is quite another matter.'

'Do you have your suspicions?'

'Very much more, Madam. I am only too well aware of the thief's identity. He is a certain Septimus Keen.'

'Septimus Keen?' Clarissa paled. 'I believe I recall the name,' she said faintly.

'I sincerely hope not, Madam. He is completely mad. His acquaintance would not profit you one whit.'

'Stories?' Clarissa suggested tentatively. 'Does he not write stories?'

'How very peculiar that you should be aware of the fact, Madam. Yes, he does write stories, and very curious and unusual stories too, which is how I came to know him. He was patronised by Dr Lipsius.'

'This is all absolutely fascinating, Mr Raymond. I have myself read two of his bizarre and outlandish tales. He was at one time a patient in an asylum, was he not?'

'I can quite believe it,' Mr Montague Raymond commented. 'Certainly he is insane. I confess to an admiration for his literary efforts, but hardly for his ethics. For many months he enjoyed the sun of Lipsius's benevolence. Then he abused it by insulting his benefactor, cheating him of his patronage, and robbing him of many items from his priceless collection. Yet despite this disgraceful conduct, Dr Lipsius remained his gentle and forgiving self. He would not hear of contacting the police, for he was quite convinced that "our poor Septimus", as he called him, had been led astray by another. He therefore begged me to act as his intermediary and discover Septimus Keen in the hope of effecting a reconciliation. After Lipsius's kindness towards me personally, I could not in all good conscience refuse.'

'I anticipate that you will have difficulty in locating Mr Septimus Keen,' Clarissa said softly. 'I gather that he is curiously elusive.'

'The correctness of your information baffles me, Madam,' replied Mr Raymond, studying her face carefully. 'For he cannot be found anywhere. He possesses the true cunning of the insane and has mastered the art of invisibility. He has become a devilish imposter.'

'A devilish imposter, Mr Raymond? This reeks rather of diablerie.'

'Diablerie pure and unsullied, Madam. For Septimus Keen must be the soul of what we call the Decadence, little realising what it is that we describe by the word. He has entirely abandoned the idea of identity. In consequence, no one knows who he is, let alone where he is.'

'Pray more champagne, Mr Raymond,' said Clarissa, opening her fan with abrupt energy. 'I think I require a glass merely to clear my head.

How, in Heaven's name, can one abandon the idea of identity?'

'It is perfectly simple, Madam. Forget who you are, and be someone else each day. Let us take Septimus Keen. On Monday, perhaps he is Major George Fortescue, on leave from India; on Tuesday, he is the Reverend Cyril Prendergast, a High Churchman from an obscure parish in Devon; Wednesday sees him as Mr Frank Kirkwood, who lives in Wimbledon and is something in the City; come Thursday he sallies forth as Otis B. Wood, an American impresario from High Plains, Wisconsin; Friday he goeth forth in the guise of Ernst Stammler, a student of Philosophy at the University of Heidelberg; the curtain of Saturday is raised to reveal Sir Anthony Cresswell, baronet, gentleman of leisure and man about town, whilst on Sunday he perchance metamorphoses into Mr Maurice Stott, a professional impersonator, now appearing at the Gaiety Theatre, Clerkenwell.'

Clarissa's hand trembled as she raised her glass of champagne. Her temples throbbed with the ache of unreality, and as she fought off a shudder, Mr Raymond relentlessly continued.

'You seem a trifle affected, Madam, but I assure you that worse is to come. I am informed that he occasionally claims to be Septimus Keen, knowing that no one will believe him, since he has persuaded several of his dubious acquaintances to make precisely the same claim. And recently he has taken to impersonating people who actually exist, to their considerable consternation, and my own. This fact I learned in a most distressing manner. I chanced the other day upon an old acquaintance of mine, a Mr Harold Sedgemoor . . .'

'Sedgemoor . . .' faltered Clarissa.

'The same. Perhaps you yourself have the good fortune of knowing this illustrious gentleman, whose arduous endeavours to maintain the proper dignity of literature are so justly appreciated by the discerning few? No? No matter. I know him well, and was enchanted by our unexpected meeting. We had lunch together, and though he struck me as being a little distant, I enjoyed his wit and conversation to an unanticipated degree. He invited me to call upon him in his rooms the following day.' Mr. Raymond sipped a little champagne. 'Well: I ask you to picture my amazement when I did so, and discovered to my considerable confusion that Mr Sedgemoor was not expecting me, that he remembered neither the invitation, nor the luncheon, nor even our encounter. He supplied me with a detailed description of where he had been when I thought I was having lunch with him, a description subsequently corroborated, and I was placed in the unenviable position of having to explain to him that I was the victim not of amnesia or hallucinations, but of the most diabolical and insolent imposture. Without realising the fact, I had lunched with Septimus Keen, who had taken what was no doubt considerable pleasure in making a fool of me. Now perhaps you comprehend my perplexity, which has been contorted by your own troubling strictures concerning the character of Dr Lipsius. It could well be that Keen has resorted to blackening the character of my esteemed friend.'

'You leave me quite flabbergasted, Mr Raymond. I no longer can be sure of anything. Only the other day, a good friend of mine encountered this Mr Sedgemoor, who was at the time occupied in fending off the attacks of foodpads. My friend rushed to his assistance, they then introduced themselves, and I believe Mr Sedgemoor kindly showed his rescuer a tale by Septimus Keen in the course of an unusual narrative in which he claimed to be a victim of a malign persecution.'

'I fear your friend has also fallen victim to a brazen deception,' Mr Raymond replied gravely. 'Harold Sedgemoor has not to my knowledge so much as heard of Septimus Keen. Moreover, this wild and dangerous young man is in the habit of regaling perfect strangers with his astonishing tales, and so there can be no question as to the fact of the imposture. Fortunately this latter habit has furnished me with a clue which may yet result in his apprehension. By tracking down each person upon whom these narratives have been inflicted, I may perhaps alight upon Keen's whereabouts. For this purpose I have at present upon my person one such tale. Like Keen, I show it to perfect strangers, and

I ask them if they have ever seen the like, hoping that chance may at length enlighten me and lead my footsteps to his dwelling-place. A curious and unusual method of detection you may think, but then I am a connoisseur in these august matters. I confess I was on the point of inviting you to peruse the peculiar tale I have here, but you have anticipated my wildest expectations.'

'Even so, Mr Raymond, I admit my curiosity. I really would rather like to read another tale from his haunting pen. What you tell me of the author fascinates as much as it repels.'

'Madam, I cannot but accede to your gracious request,' said Mr Raymond, with a courtesy that stopped just short of unction. He plucked a neat manuscript from his inside breast pocket and handed it to Clarissa. 'This tale,' he added, 'is all the more riveting for me because it concerns the artist, Francis Melsomm, whose work is one of my abiding passions. He appears in the narrative as Robert Ashe.'

Clarissa paid scant heed to his words as she hastily opened the manuscript and proceeded to read:

THE DEVIL'S MAZE

'Let it not be supposed by those who read me that I am the victim of hallucinations brought on by dint of continued excess. My mind is only too well awake with a cold lucidity. Its powers are perhaps the major barrier between myself and genius, for if genius is controlled insanity, I am ever the victim of my own control. I have tried by many means to break it down, I confess, but my measure of success has been small, and so I stare at those who have succeeded in their art with an amalgam of envy, admiration, and incomprehension. My untempered sanity, I fear, will be only too evident in the tale I have to tell, for it concerns one who has succeeded where I have failed, and contains too the reason for his success and my failure, and makes me despair of the possibility of ever arriving at the end of my desperate journey.

'So much for the introduction, which was necessary only to stress the strength of my rational perceptions. I can now begin to tell you about my friend, Robert Ashe. With his appearance we are not especially concerned. It is enough to say that he was a young man of slender build and of a retiring disposition. Rather more germane is the fact that he was an artist.

'It was at the house of Madame D'Estelle that I first encountered him. She was an expatriate Parisian widow, an eccentric lady, who used to give soirées to which only those concerned with the contemporary development of the arts were ever invited. For Madame D'Estelle saw herself as the inspired high priestess of a movement which elsewhere has received the appellation of the Decadence.

She made no secret of the fact that she had known the renowned French Magician, Eliphas Levi, and to her inner circle confided the fact that she had assisted him in the performance of a ritual which had as its aim nothing less than the destruction of our stale civilisation and its eventual regeneration. She firmly believed that the success of this ritual was daily making itself felt, and that artists were the prophets of its victory.

'She spoke of the magicians who had nurtured the initial results of the spell, Gerard Encausse, Stanislas De Guiata, Sar Peladan, and the English Order Of The Golden Dawn. She spoke of painters such as Moreau and Redon, of poets such as Baudelaire and Verlaine, of novelists such as Toulet and Huysmans. These were the high priests beneath her, and below these came those English artists who had felt the rapture of the spell, and who, when they visited, were welcomed with impressive solemnity.

'And so I too came to sing the wild songs of Swinburne, to dream over the bejewelled prose of Pater, to feel the moonbeam ripple of Wilde's epigrams tingle upon my skin, to weep the tears of a deliciously insincere repentance over the exquisitely sinful line of Aubrey Beardsley.

'Never shall I forget those soirées of Madame D'Estelle, when the guiding spirits of the age graced the luxurious salon with their presence and my eager ears with their mad wisdom. Some sat enthroned upon a fearsome reputation, others embraced an obscurity that they might better let their minds' shadow play seep into the fabric of their creations. I think I perhaps preferred these latter to, for instance, the mystic Celtic twilight that enshrouded William Butler Yeats, or the coldly complacent revolt that emanated from George Moore. Instead I sought out those who scorned to shelter beneath a public persona, such as Arthur Machen, an exquisite novelist of modest reputation, and Aleister Crowley, a Cambridge undergraduate of impressive brilliance. One with whom I found instant communion was Robert Ashe.

'At that time he was sustained by a meagre private income, but he endured all privations without the slightest resentment. He had only one desire in this life, and that was to paint. To paint with the artistry to which he aspired, he openly avowed, there was nothing that he would not do. His body he esteemed little, alternatively torturing it with rigorous asceticism and the most demanding debauchery. His mind he perhaps esteemed even less, for he cheerfully contemplated the possibility of a sacrifice of sanity, informing me that all that held him back was the suspicion that the result might be permanently damaging to his craftsmanship.

'It will readily be understood that such single-minded dedication evoked in me an irrepressible desire to witness its fruits. After an initial hesitancy, he at last acceded to my request, and I can clearly recall the excitement with which I followed him up the flights of stairs that led to the garret which he occupied in a dilapidated house in Kensal Rise. The uncarpeted room contained a bed, a wash-basin and no more, apart from its wealth of paintings which littered the floorboards, rendering it difficult to move unimpeded. Then was I at last able to witness the early work of the remarkable Robert Ashe.

'I had expected to look upon a universe of devils and angels, sinless youths about to taste the delights of casual corruption, women worn with the work of wickedness. I saw none of this. Instead I saw intricate patterns of line, form and colour, which took me quite aback with their singular symmetry and harmony. Technically, his work was faultless, and exhibited a craftsmanship which I have yet to see paralleled. Every brush stroke was guided by a central purpose, every colour contributed its exaltation to the balanced whole. Our sternest and most pedantic academic critics could not have found fault with the minutest particle of each painting. And yet what I saw was not the stuff from which great art nourishes its being.

'We stood in silence for a few moments.

' "Your imagination has far outstripped the reality, I fear." Robert Ashe spoke at last. "You possibly expected art devoid of the very slightest standards of craftsmanship, and you find in its place craftsmanship devoid of art.''

'I made no reply. There was none that I could make. Presently he spoke again, and every word he spoke will remain to torment me.

''For me, patience is the secret of great art. Inspiration rarely visits those who summon her as one would a servant. Our task is to await her coming with fortitude, and in the meanwhile to perfect ourselves as instruments. What you see here is but the uninteresting product of a labour that has no object save its own perfectability. I paint patterns, mazes, labyrinths as I await my redemption. My skill has only one purpose: to create the perfect maze. When I have done so, the Devil will find his way to me and grant me all that I desire. Then, and only then, will inspiration be my faithful servant, for no power on earth, in heaven or in hell can stand against that unleashed by the sacrifice of a soul.''

' ''I had thought,'' I ventured in reply, ''that the Devil comes readily enough to those who can call him with their whole will.''

' ''Their whole will!'' he exclaimed. ''Have you the smallest idea of what that means? Myself, I have never met a man or woman who was in possession of anything that could remotely be called a whole will. Every mortal is a democracy of shifting moods. But these patterns that you see possess as their ultimate purpose the preparation of a will from which everything untidy and extraneous has been mercilessly banished. I know that my paintings lack what you may call 'soul'. For with each one I rid myself of an impeding and inessential obsession. I seek to cleanse myself in order that the soul I will ultimately summon will be the Devil, and nothing but the Devil, who may then seize upon my purity and mate it with his own glutted sensuality, that the offspring may be the truth of artistic greatness before which even God Himself bows down. I aspire to the light that my embrace with the Devil may be so explosive that entire universes are by it rent and cast asunder. My work nears its end. Soon I will call him.''

'I could not reply, for no words could delimit the totality of my response. I thanked him confusedly, and stumbled from his garret, dazed and afflicted. For many hours afterwards I paced the pavements in a fever of perturbation. I dared not return to my own work, in which an imagination which was only in part inspired, wrestled with innumerable deficiencies of execution. I feared lest the well from which I drank my creative sustenance was impure and unclean, or lest my presumption in attempting artistry be compared by the gods to the prattling of an intelligent ape.

'And even weeks afterwards, the words of Robert Ashe hampered all my attempts to write. I was appalled by the way in which words mastered me rather than I them. I was tormented by the feeble nature of the inspiration upon which sentences fed, and found therein the strength to obsess me. To write well became an impossible ideal.

'All attempts to bludgeon the imagination now became as vain as I had always inwardly suspected them to be. I found myself despising all inspiration but the ultimate, and that declined to show its visage to me. Then I endeavoured to acquire technical perfection, hoping by the means of Robert Ashe to find relief. In busy succession I penned Petrarchan sonnets, mythological epics in rhyming couplets, drama in blank verse, social comedy, naturalistic short story, symboliste odes and penny dreadfuls. These were distinguished both by their facility and by their lifelessness.

'I began to despair, contemplating even the abandoning of literature in favour of journalism. But I had always talked to myself of artistic perfection, and I clung to my belief that here I was entirely devoid of hypocrisy and affectation. The weeks passed, and I continued upon my quest, but my slipshod manner was now so sternly corrected that I barely succeeded in writing one page. It was when I had degenerated into attempts to write a perfect sentence, and a confrontation with my inability to do so, that I decided that I could unburden my struggle to one other person who, knowing its tortures, might well console me and sharpen my resolve.

'I made my way to the garret of Robert Ashe as

though I was an apprentice seeking the counsel of his Master. I ascended the stairway with unsure tread, unsure of what my reception might be. With mingled awe and admiration, I knocked upon the wooden surface of the door.

' "Yes," said a voice, in a tone of sweet simplicity.

'I opened the door, entered stealthily, and closed it behind me. Robert Ashe was seated, cross-legged upon the floor. His eyes were closed, and he barely seemed to be breathing. Upon his face was an expression of supreme peace.

' "I called him," he said, "and he came."

'Before him was an easel upon which stood a painting. The oil was still moist. It was an arrangement of colour, form and line. Each element formed part of an intricate labyrinth, each part of which led on to another. The picture had neither beginning nor end, for one started with one part and was drawn to another endlessly through a splash and foam of sublime artistry. As I vibrated in my contemplation of the whole, I perceived more, and everything seemed to draw back, until I could not be sure whether I was seeing whole or part of the picture.

'It happened. One moment I was looking at the picture, and then I was the picture. I saw a flame which devoured all who dared approach it. I heard the whisper of a shadow that beckoned me to my destruction. I smelt the stink of death as it hovered just behind me. I tasted a blood that flowed freely from those mortals whom the gods have sacrificed. I felt the wings of eternity kiss my giving lips. I was borne along the current I had unwittingly unleashed. I became the maze I had entered.

'I may have wandered countless aeons amidst insane geometry. Voices whispered to me of a thread, and then I plucked it from the ground and followed its absurd meanderings. It could not lead me to the maze's entrance, for there was no entrance since the entrance was nowhere. But it could lead me to the maze's centre, in the instant that I realised that the centre was everywhere.

'And then I knew I had arrived at the end of my Quest, for I was the Quest. May my soul be preserved from what I saw, though it undergo beforehand an eternity of torment!

'For I beheld the Devil.

'He smiled at me. He extended one arm upon which was tattooed the price of my soul, and another which revealed a cosmos of artistic genius, in which the Universe breathed within a book that danced before my eyes and bore my name.

' ''Yes,'' said a voice, in a tone of sweet simplicity.

'His eyes were closed, and he barely seemed to be breathing. Upon his face was an expression of supreme peace.

' ''You called me,'' he said, ''and I came.''

'I screamed my denial. I shrank from his welcoming claw. I called upon all that was rational to protect me. And I fled from the sight of the Devil. I cannot tell how long I stumbled through his maze, for I suspect that I have never left it.

'I remember things. A painting. The radiant face of Robert Ashe. A door. A bed. A clock upon my wall. A pad of paper. A pen.

'That is all I have to say concerning Robert Ashe, for now I know the secret of his genius. Since that time I have shunned his company with a terror that is more than mortal. I have obstinately clung to my continued sanity, and the powers of my mind persist in impeding the appearance of genius.

'I am still fleeing from the Devil. I have been so rash as to invoke him with my whole will, and then spurn his offer. My nights are filled with my attempts to break free from his maze, the maze which he is. I know I cannot fight him long, and that soon will be forced upon me both genius and my sacrifice. For I cannot in the end but surrender, since upon the Devil's face I saw my own.

Clarissa folded the manuscript very slowly, and handed it to Mr Raymond very quickly.

'Yes,' she heard herself say clearly, 'it is obviously the work of Septimus Keen. You, Mr Raymond, if I may speak freely, are a curious and unusual connoisseur. If I were in your place, I would abandon my search for the author. For even if you were to discover him, which I now think supremely unlikely, I fail to see what good this would do the ethics which you mentioned earlier.'

'My ethics and my sense of honour, Madam, compel me to assist Dr Lipsius, who has, after all, favoured me with his invaluable help in my researches. My ethics compel me also to rescue Septimus Keen from the mercenary female who has made of his creative lunacy something that is malevolent.'

Clarissa drained her champagne glass in one nervous gulp.

'I sincerely hope,' she said very firmly, 'that she is not a young lady with flaming red hair, for whom so many ingenious persons are searching.'

'I feel I shall go quite, quite mad,' declared Mr Raymond. 'I am indeed also looking for the young lady you describe, but I did not suspect she was so much sought after. I know very little of her, but I feel she will be easier to find than her unfortunate paramour whose misplaced cunning she so deftly encourages. You have not by any chance seen her perhaps? I am told she moves in the very highest social circles.'

Clarissa ignored the implied compliment and rose with a sudden action that betokened the appearance of unshakable resolve.

'It has been a curious and unusual lunch, Mr Raymond. I thank you for your kindness and courtesy. Now kindly escort me to my carriage.'

'Madam, I hope I have not in some way offended your delicate sensibility . . .?'

'Not at all. I feel a trifle unwell, and I do believe that if I am not within my carriage very shortly, I shall faint.'

'Very well, permit me to attend to the insignificant trifle of our bill of fare. I apologise for having spoken so bluntly.'

Clarissa waved aside his apologies, and moments later he was escorting her to the carriage that had followed the cab they had taken from the old curiosity shop. He helped her in with the utmost propriety, then began his farewell address.

'Rarely, Madam, has a little refreshment proved more richly rewarding . . .'

'My sentiments also, Mr Raymond,' Clarissa cut in hastily. 'I wish you every success. Forgive me, but circumstances compel me to say farewell.'

With that, she waved him aside and the carriage drew away. She glanced briefly behind her, and saw that he was still regarding the carriage, as smooth, smiling and clean-shaven as he had been earlier that day. Then she settled back into the cushions of the vehicle, while her gloved fingers searched for an elusive cigarette. The gates that led to another world had opened wider, and her mind staggered away from their eerie welcome. As if to consolidate her hold upon common things, she invoked the spectres of social conventions through whose eyes it was easier to analyse her perturbing experience. Montague Raymond's story at times had resounded with a certain tuneful conviction yet there remained an uneasy sense of mendacious orchestration.

And it was with a definite chill that she recalled that neither Henry Potter, nor Arabella Wesley, nor Montague Raymond had so much as ventured to ask her her name.

8

The Enchantress of St John's Woods

(The Image That Counts)

Nine days after Clarissa's meeting with the unfortunate Mrs Wesley in the Savoy, Charles Renshawe was standing in the very same hotel, sipping a glass of fine old claret. It was now half-past eight in the evening, and Renshawe had been there an hour, hoping that either the hotel or the wine would inspire him with a solution to the puzzle of the young lady with flaming red hair.

'I cannot make any sense of it either,' Clarissa had told him the previous evening. 'Three most ingenious people are for some mysterious reason searching for this lady, whose mortal existence we have ourselves ascertained, and it seems that they require her company sufficiently to relate to us certain remarkable narratives, which include tales by one Mr Septimus Keen, whose existence upon this earth is still a matter of conjecture.'

'Style,' Renshawe had replied. 'Style. It is all in the style of Lipsius. This chain of events is so bizarre, the man must be involved, but I confess I have not the remotest notion of how or why.'

He sighed heavily, finished his glass, discovered that the solution to the puzzle did not lie in its dregs, doubted whether it would be at the bottom of another, and decided to leave the hotel. It was a fine October night, and he resolved upon walking home. As he neared Piccadilly Circus, he observed with detached interest the bustle at the heart of the Empire, whose rulers possessed wealth which Nero would not have despised. The pavements were crowded with smartly dressed men about town and others who were aping them, and ladies, whose apparel cost more than most earned in a year, passed by with their husbands, escorts and chaperones in gleaming black cabs and carriages. At the Haymarket, the number of unattended ladies on foot increased sharply, and some of them plucked at Renshawe's sleeve. These, he knew, were but a fraction of the sixty thousand 'soiled doves' who plied their trade in London, and he was unsurprised by the fact that many seemed not much older than fourteen.

It was as though he had entered a region in which all the inhabitants were compelled to sport cheap finery and plaster their worn faces with lashings of paint and grease. With a slight shudder, he brushed aside the grasping fingers that implored his custom, and was about to cross the road when a woman whispered in his ear.

'Sir, I am not what I seem. I beg you, assist a lady in distress. I want not your wallet but your protection.'

Renshawe turned to regard a young woman in a shimmering purple evening gown and ermine wrap, with masses of black curls, and hazel eyes that shone imploringly from a quaint and piquant face.

'I beg your pardon . . .' he began, unsure as to whether or not this was some new business tactic of a lady of pleasure, but was deterred from striding onward by an expression of panic which abruptly etched itself upon the woman's face.

'Come,' she urgently insisted, seizing him by the arm. 'Another moment of delay and my enemies will be upon me!' Any hesitation which still tempted Renshawe was instantly brushed aside by her ensuing words. 'I pray you, keep a sharp lookout for a lady with flaming red hair. Should she espy me here, I fear my days are numbered.'

That was all that Renshawe needed. Seconds later, he had hailed a cab and bundled inside both the terrified young lady and himself, and had commanded the cabman to drive in a northerly direction.

'Sir, I do not know how I can thank you,' said the woman. 'I realise fully how peculiar this must all seem, but I assure you, your conduct is of the utmost chivalry. I knew that you were a courageous gentleman the moment I set eyes upon you. May I warn you that my enemies are entirely without scruple, and would not hesitate to assault a lady? Please keep your eyes open for anything in the smallest degree suspicious.'

'Madam,' said a nonplussed Charles Renshawe,

'much as I am desirous of assisting a lady in distress, I would nevertheless be grateful for some form of explanation.'

'Later, later,' answered the lady. 'For the present, I urge you to be vigilant. Above all, tell me if you espy my deadly and unrelenting foe. She is a striking woman. You cannot miss her flaming red hair.'

'This is . . . a singularly fortunate encounter,' replied Renshawe as his brain worked furiously. 'Permit me to introduce myself. Robert Bastin, private investigator, who is engaged upon a search for the very woman you describe.'

'Indeed,' the lady commented thoughtfully. 'Then I think we shall have much to say to one another, Mr Bastin. My name is Deborah Mornington,' she extended a white-gloved hand, 'and I suggest you accompany me· to my home in St John's Wood. Once we reach safety, we can discuss this affair in the privacy which it so definitely requires.'

'That proposal, Miss Mornington, has my un-qualified assent.'

'In the meantime, continue your scrutinising of the streets. We are not yet safe.' Miss Mornington gave him a final piercing glance, then turned her head in the direction of Oxford Street, to her right.

The cab continued in a northerly direction, up Baker Street, then past Regent's Park until it reached St John's Wood, whereupon it journeyed through a series of sidestreets before finally halting outside a small but desirable residence. Miss Mornington looked once more behind her, as if to ascertain whether they were being pursued, then descended to the pavement, allowing Renshawe to pay the cabman.

The house was furnished with evident opulence, and the drawing room into which the lady led Renshawe was littered with many curious *objets d'art*, some of which would have elicited frowns from respectable women and clergymen.

'A glass of port, Mr Bastin?'

'That would be delightful, Miss Mornington. Do you live here by yourself?'

'I do. I have always found solitude to be congenial. Now then, Mr Bastin,' she cast off her wrap and flung herself into a chaise-longue, 'tell me of your involvement with the red-haired lady.'

Renshawe sipped his port, which was agreeably sweet and strong, as he hunted within his mind for a series of lies which he hoped would prove convincing.

'There is not very much to tell, Miss Mornington. I was only employed this morning, and by the agent of a person who desired to remain anonymous. I was given a handsome sum, and informed that more would be forthcoming if only I could discover the whereabouts of a certain young lady, who, for reasons which I do not understand, uses a variety of alibis and resides at many different addresses. I gather that she had means at her disposal, and I decided to commence my mission by exploring London's hotels, hoping that I might chance upon her, but I must confess that my search has hitherto been a fruitless one.'

'Oh,' said Miss Mornington, as if disappointed. 'Do you know nothing else about her?'

'It appears that I am being kept almost entirely in ignorance. However, those who are engaged in the occupation I have chosen must learn to bear the secrecy of those who employ them. I heartily wish I possessed one fraction of the powers of Mr Sherlock Holmes, whose exploits in the pages of *The Strand* magazine are so capably narrated by the celebrated Conan Doyle, for it seems that my task will be a hard one.'

'Well, well, well,' mused Miss Mornington. 'I had not realised that there are those who hope to lay hands upon the woman whom I fear with such just cause. I am very pleased indeed to make your acquaintance, Mr Bastin, for it seems that I have encountered a gentleman who may assist me further just when it seemed that all was lost. Would you like me to tell you why I flee from the woman whom you seek? I am sure that we are speaking of the same individual.'

'That would be very good of you,' Renshawe answered.

'Not at all. More port, Mr Bastin?'

'Thank you. It is very good.'

'My pleasure entirely. It is good that you are a

private detective, for you will not be shocked at anything I might say. Hitherto my words of truth have perhaps been fewer than is desirable, for, Mr Bastin,' the lady fluttered her eyelids demurely, 'I am what is called a courtesan. In plainer language, I am a very expensive prostitute, and I perform my services for the rich which grant them a release from the tribulations of politics, commerce and industry, and hence I contribute to the health and well-being of our society. I am not ashamed of my occupation. My parents were possessed of little wealth, and this form of pleasurable labour struck me as being the only way in which I could live in the style I desired while preserving my independence. You may regard me as you would a Harley Street specialist in mental aberrations.'

'Your attitude might be called unusual, Miss Mornington,' Renshawe commented politely.

'Possibly, Mr Bastin, but then I flatter myself that I am an unusual woman. To continue: about twelve months ago, I received as a client a young man who told me that his name was Septimus Keen. In the months that followed, I was to learn that he was the nephew of a prominent member of the Government; perhaps this is the anonymous gentleman who has seen fit to employ you. At any rate, Septimus Keen had abandoned the promise of a public career in favour of the less remunerative but no doubt more satisfying pastime of literature. Although possessed of substantial funds, he affected an abysmal poverty, presumably in order to observe life.

'His requirements were not unusual to one such as myself. He was a member of that fast increasing class of men which looks upon women as the superior sex. Indeed, my income informs me that this attitude is reaching the proportions of an epidemic, and it will not surprise me if in the not too distant future, women take openly to the wearing of trousers. I see you frown, Mr Bastin; no matter; time alone will tell. The fact remains that Septimus Keen desired my discipline and domination. Possibly you have encountered works of literature describing this kind of relationship? I would mention: *Venus In Furs, Gynaeocracy, Miss High Heels, The Petticoat Dominant; Or Woman's Revenge* and *The Mistress And The Slave*. He paid me well for punishing him by putting him in ladies' petticoats, and as for my whip . . .'

'Miss Mornington!' broke in Renshawe, who had become quite perturbed by the lady's descriptive relish, 'Are these details absolutely essential?'

'No, but it is interesting, is it not, that his illustrious uncle possesses similar tastes? You see, he is also a client of mine. But I can see that you have no desire to hear of my sweet little torture-chamber and similar delights of 'self-expression,' Miss Mornington emitted a loud peal of laughter at Renshawe's obvious discomfiture. 'I will carry on with my narrative. The uncle informed me that

Septimus was for him the source of acute embarrassment, and that he intended to resolve the
situation. I endeavoured both to dissuade him, and
to warn the young man, but despite my efforts, the
nephew was seized six months ago, and incarcerated in a private lunatic asylum. I was very sorry
to hear of this. He was a most generous client.

'I continued to pleasure the uncle, and only
recently did I learn from him that Septimus had
escaped with the aid of the woman you seek.
Obviously, I did not share the man's anger. Indeed,
I felt quite pleased for Septimus, and wondered at
the identity of his helper, who, I gathered, was
possessed of a magnificent head of flaming red
hair. Then, this very morning, to my intense
consternation, I received a letter from Septimus.'
Miss Mornington produced a letter from her bag,
and read:

'Darling Deborah, my darling delight, please
forgive my haste. I am involved in events the
import of which lies far beyond my comprehension.
I have been kidnapped by a cruel and ruthless
woman. To this, as you know, I have no objection,
but I fear for your own safety. For reasons of
politics and espionage which I do not understand,
she is bent upon your assassination, and insists
that you are in the possession of vital information
as a result of knowing me. Burn this letter and
beware! Your adoring Septimus.'

'Mr Bastin, you can well imagine my state of

pitiable anguish. I am but a lady of business. To be threatened with murder is a terrifying prospect!'

'How extraordinary,' murmured Renshawe. 'Why on earth would this lady think you were in possession of information?'

'That I cannot fathom. The only thing I can think of is a manuscript which Septimus gave me. I was under the impression that it was one of those bizarre tales which he writes, but now the possibility occurs to me that it contains some kind of coded message.'

'May I see it?'

'By all means.' Miss Mornington extracted a manuscript from her bag and handed Renshawe the tale of:

THE IMAGE THAT COUNTS

'The first time it happened, Oliver Gray suffered his first serious doubts concerning his sanity.

'Eight o'clock in the morning is not a suitable time to ponder such matters, but Gray really had no choice. For it began at that singularly helpless period of the morning when one first tentatively glances in the mirror. Gray regarded his image. It was unshaven, bleary-eyed, and grinning.

'Which is when the horrible truth struck him that he himself was not grinning at all.

'He pinched himself; the image did likewise; he was not dreaming. He winked, but the image refused to respond. He smiled; the image scowled. He waved his arms; the image seemed to sneer. He shouted; the image regarded him impassively.

'Wholly unnerved by the encounter, white-faced and trembling, Gray stumbled into the kitchen and poured himself a very large whisky. He gulped it down voraciously and returned to his looking glass.

'He grimaced; the image smiled. He yelled; the image continued to smile. He screamed; the image yawned. He left the room and returned with an axe; the image laughed. It was still laughing as Gray hacked the glass into a thousand pieces.

2

' "Miss Simpson!" Gray called from within the office. "Could you possibly come in here one moment, please?"

'The lady in the outer office wearily rose, and entered the inner sanctum of the Chief Sales Manager. He looked white and ill.

' "Thank you," said Gray, his voice shaking as the woman entered. "Thank you. Now—ah—could you just watch the mirror for a few moments . . . and my face . . . just curious about something that has occurred, that's all . . ."

'She nodded dumbly.

'Gray scowled; the image scowled back. Gray smiled; and so did the image.

' "Will that be all, Mr Gray?" the woman asked impatiently.

' "Odd, very odd," Gray muttered to himself, "I could've sworn that . . ." he cleared his throat, "ahem, you didn't—well—perceive any—er—difference, did you Miss Simpson, between—well—between my face and the looking-glass . . .?"

' "No," said the woman, quite mystified. "It is a mirror, after all, Mr Gray."

' "Yes, yes, yes. Of course. You are quite correct. A mirror. Thank you Miss Simpson, that will be all."

'How peculiar, thought the woman as she left the room. He must be feeling ill. Very odd indeed. As they say, keeping up appearances can be a strain.

3

'Gray broke down that afternoon. Wherever he went, there had been polished surfaces, and wherever there had been polished surfaces, there was his reflection, smiling regardless of whether Gray was smiling or not. Except when others regarded the reflection. Then the image would once more become servile.

'Gray was found by the Managing Director attacking his office looking-glass with a hammer. He was calmed, given a sedative, and sent home. In the glass window of his front door, his reflection winked at him.

4

'There was only one conceivable course of action for Oliver Gray. He decided to confront his image, and subdue it by an act of sheer will power. Half a bottle of brandy nerved him for the contest.

'The man regarded his reflection for a long time. At last, as if to acknowledge the man's superiority, the image grinned ruefully.

'To his intense horror and disgust, Gray found that he was grinning ruefully too.

'The image winked; so did he. The image laughed; he did also. The image waved, and he waved back. The image tapped its temple with its first finger and shook its head; Gray gave up the struggle and obeyed.

'The eyes of the image seemed to widen. Grey could not but stare into them. The figure seemed to blur as Gray found himself being sucked towards it.

5

'Something very like a switch seemed to click in Gray's benumbed brain, and he found himself once more regarding a clear image. Then the reflection smiled once more, and turned, and Gray copied it, and was left, his back to the mirror, staring at the room.

'It was not a room he was familiar with.

229

'He was in a vast hall, the inside of a globe that seemed to encompass all eternity within it, one huge and perfect curved mirror.

'He screamed, and the scream was soundless. His fists beat against the polished surface, but failed to make even the slightest impression. Glimpses of familiar scenes, streets, his home, his office, were reflected from various parts of the globe's interior.

'He could see his image now, walking along the street that led to his office. Terror-stricken, yet enraged, Gray slid along the shining surface in an effort to confront it.

'The image turned, and saw him, and smiled, well-dressed, confident, handsome, opulent, he saw Gray and he smiled. An expression which veiled any thoughts or feelings; he smiled.

'And Gray, with an inward shudder, realised he was smiling too.'

'This is a most absorbing and provoking tale,' said Renshawe, 'but I cannot discern any kind of coded message. He handed back the manuscript, feeling oppressed by the perfumed stuffiness of the room, and by the peculiar character of its occupant. His temples throbbed with a dull ache. The port had been unusually strong.

'Alas, Mr Bastin!' cried Miss Mornington. 'What can I do? Can you suggest anything at all? I am really quite desperate!'

'Yes, Madam, you are, and I can indeed suggest a remedy,' Renshawe riposted, wishing that his headache was gone. 'I suggest that we unmask. I am not Mr Bastin, and you are not Deborah Mornington. Let us bring the curtain down upon this little masquerade.' He produced a pistol from his coat pocket, and placed it on the table in front of him, noting with some surprise that the young lady seemed wholly unperturbed. 'I wish to hear the unvarnished truth about the red-haired lady and Mr Septimus Keen whom you and your confederates are hunting.'

'What a clever man you are!' laughed the girl.

'Kindly do not insult me with flattery,' Renshawe said thickly. 'We are quite alone here. I intend to have the truth by fair means or foul.'

'That,' replied the young woman, 'remains to be seen.'

As she spoke, Renshawe felt the room swim giddily before his aching eyes. He tried to focus, and to shut out the roaring that had started in his ears, but his stomach seemed to turn a somersault each time he gasped for air. A red mist imposed itself on his awareness, then blackness descended, and he pitched forward onto the white carpet, unconscious.

'A most artistic end to a Blood Quest,' Helen murmured quietly, 'though I feared the drug would never take effect. Another glass of port, Mr Renshawe?' She rose, knelt down by the body, and began to strip it of its clothing. 'Farewell, Miss Mornington, and farewell, Mrs Wesley. Welcome, Mr Charles Renshawe. Dr Lipsius will be delighted to make your acquaintance. You poor fool, did you not realise that our dramas were enacted entirely for your benefit, to snare you in a web of mental delusion. You thought you were the hunter, and when you awake, you will find to your cost that you were all the time the hunted, a mouse with whom cats toyed. A stylish denouement, is it not, Mr Renshawe?' she cooed as she pulled away his underpants. 'Oh yes,' she added gaily, 'I think that will do nicely for the doctor's museum.'

9

Strange Occurrence in Kensington

(The History of the Young Lady with Flaming Red Hair)

'As a man of liberal persuasion,' said Lord Selkirk, 'I am certainly concerned about the problem of the poor. Indeed, it is surely obvious to any thinking person that the solution lies in the encouragement of habits of industry and thrift.'

He sat back impressively, cradling a glass of fine old burgundy in his hand, and gazed at Lady Clarissa Mountford. The dinner party was into its second hour and its fourth course. Turtle soup had been succeeded by sole, and then by partridge, and the dozen guests were now enjoying beef, which would be followed by puddings, of various descriptions, Devils on Horseback as a savoury, cheese, and fruit, and ultimately tea and cakes. All courses were of course accompanied by appropriate wines, all of the rarest vintage.

'This is precisely why I find the theories of Mr Bernard Shaw to be abhorrent and pernicious. He succeeds only in making the poor feel dissatisfied, and the more foolish of the rich feel guilty,' Lord Selkirk continued. 'Nor do I esteem him as a dramatist or critic. His work is meretricious, and what little success it has enjoyed is due purely to the vagaries of public taste. In a hundred years time, he will be quite forgotten, I assure you, as the unlamented Oscar Wilde is now.'

'Whom, in your considered opinion, will be remembered?' asked Clarissa, as she endeavoured to stifle a yawn.

'Surely that is obvious? Writers of real worth will be remembered, like Mr Hall Caine, Mrs Oliphant, Mr Marion Crawford and Mr Henry Arthur Jones, and certainly Mrs Humphrey Ward. But to return to the problem of the poor . . .'

But Clarissa was not to be granted the pleasure of listening to the views of Lord Selkirk on this particular evening, for the butler had bent down, and was muttering some words into her ear.

'Pray excuse me,' announced Clarissa as she rose from her chair. 'I have just received news of some matters which compel my immediate attention.'

She swept from the room, the butler following at her heels, and stepping ahead only to open the door for Her Ladyship. As she reached her private study on the ground floor of her Kensington mansion, she permitted a frown to inscribe itself upon her features.

'Well, Alfred? Where is the package which the young lady delivered?'

'Here, Your Ladyship,' replied the butler, giv-

ing her a large white envelope which reposed upon
a silver tray.

'Bring me a large glass of brandy,' commanded
Clarissa, 'and continue to serve the guests as if
nothing has occurred.'

'Very good, Your Ladyship.'

Clarissa tore open the envelope as the butler
departed. She had in fact told her guests the truth:
that she had received news of some matters which
compelled her immediate attention. Apparently, a
young lady had called, and requested the butler to
bring an envelope to the immediate attention of Lady
Mountford, insisting that it concerned the personal
safety, not only of her Ladyship, but also that of a
Mr Charles Renshawe. The butler had described the
mysterious visitor, who had refused to give her
name, as being of pretty, if haughty appearance,
with remarkable green eyes, and flaming red hair.

Clarissa's heart began to pound when she saw that
the contents of the envelope consisted of a manuscript. She was familiar with the spidery, feminine
handwriting: it was that of the author who called
himself Septimus Keen. The brandy arrived, and
Clarissa swallowed half at one voracious gulp.
Then, as the butler departed, she proceeded to read:

THE HISTORY OF THE YOUNG LADY WITH FLAMING RED HAIR

'My name is unimportant. I am known to some as
Veronica Parke, and to others by my pen-name of

Septimus Keen. I am the lady with flaming red hair for whom so many are searching.

'Although I am of noble birth, my family is not germane to my narrative. Let it suffice to say that upon attaining the age of my majority, I quarrelled with my parents over a certain matter regarding morals, which led to an irrevocable breach, and in consequence of which I left my home, never again to return. The generosity of deceased relatives fortunately proved ample enough to sustain me in a life of comfort and independence, which I have enjoyed for the last nine years.

'Now, you cannot hope to understand me unless you realise that I believe myself to be mad. Certainly to all outward appearances I am sane enough, but my mind possesses very little in common with that of most human beings. We live in a strange age, which cannot long endure, and the more sensitive among us are aware that the *fin de siècle* is its swansong. Although the self-proclaimed prophets of our society envisage a future which progresses inevitably towards a peaceful perfection, all true artists know that we are but on the verge of the destruction of all we call civilisation. I believe that one thing is true concerning Christianity: that the next century will see the onslaught of the Four Horsemen of the Apocalypse, War, Plague, Famine and Pestilence, and the arising of the Beast and his Scarlet Woman.

'Peculiar currents pervade the atmosphere of our

age, and I have greedily imbibed their poison. I have feasted upon the works of those whom we call decadent, and my deepest desire has been to penetrate to the uttermost limits of perversity. I think I can claim to have succeeded. As a result, you might think me mad, but being mad, I do not care.

'I believe that there lie within us visions, and powers and passions which we consciously know nothing of. At times, the veil parts, and we become aware. When this awareness is permanent, this is what I call insanity, which is why I say that all true artists are insane. My art is an exploration of insanity; my life is the experience of insanity, which I realise through the unashamed pursuit of perverse pleasures. For if it is true that the saint can come to know God through asceticism and mortification of the flesh, then it is also true that the sinner may come to know God through the unabashed indulgence in debauchery. For the Devil is merely the hindquarters of God.

'My writings have never been published, though I was once foolish enough to strive in this direction, adopting a pseudonym so as to preserve my anonymity. I soon realised that publishers and editors lack the smallest semblance of awareness. Since I am not reduced to the deplorable situation of having to earn my daily bread by my pen, and since I believe myself to be the best judge of my work, I do not suffer from the pangs of neglect.

'We turn now to my pleasures. A wise man once remarked that it is very easy to call demons, for they are always calling you, and that to call the Devil, it is only necessary to call him with your whole Will. I have found this to be perfectly true. I found no shortage of societies in London which are pledged to the pursuit of diabolical pleasures, and all of them cried out for the company of an attractive and high-born young lady. I have therefore experienced no difficulty in participating in every permutation of debauchery, blasphemy and perversion.

'It is a vulgar commonplace that too much pleasure can be cloying. It was inevitable that I would weary of the tame delights of dissipation, and seek experiences of greater pungency. In the course of my quest, I encountered a certain Dr Lipsius, who proved to be the answer to my prayers.

'Lipsius is a worshipper of Darkness, one who finds the perfume of power preferable to the fresh winds of liberty, one who finds ecstasy not so much in the soft touch of pleasure, but in the savage grip of pain, the pain of others. To his disciples he reveals the abhorred mysteries of statanism, the accursed visions of Nero and Caligula, the laughterful caress of Hell's own worm. Men and women who would suit him in the service of his designs are caught like flies within his web, and he savours each juicy morsel. I relished the work I did for him, and revelled in the celebrations

of the Sabbath, when the wine of the Red Jar of
Avallaunius boiled in my veins, and I soared beyond
the pylons of time and space to embrace a being
of splendour and corruption that was, in a deeper
sense, my inmost self. Do not raise a pious eyebrow in surprise. I am mad, and claim the immuni-
ties of my affliction.

'There are those who would condemn this glorious sorcery of sin. More pertinent, there are in
existence certain fraternities which are pledged to
the Light, and whose oath it is to destroy utterly
societies like that of Dr Lipsius. Six months ago it
was rumoured that one of these Fraternities had
launched against us one of its foremost Adepts, a
man of strength and determination, who would
bend his will to the task of our eradication.

'His name was Charles Renshawe, and he was
not a man with whom we would find it easy to
trifle. He is a fine shot, and an able swordsman,
and hence any form of straight-forward physical
assault was quite out of the question. Nor was it
even theoretically possible to terminate his existence by means of a simple bullet from the rifle of
a hidden assassin, for this would run contrary to
Lipsius's commitment to the idea of style.

'The doctrine of style is simple. It consists of
the proposition that life without style is as unappetising a proposition as a pint of flat Fourpenny
Ale, and that in consequence, even the most trivial
acts must be stylish. It follows that the doom of

241

Charles Renshawe had to be engineered with subtlety and extreme artistry.

'This not undemanding task in the aesthetics of murder was given to the three foremost disciples of Lipsius: a languid gentleman of the name of Davies, who is unrivalled for his unaffected calm; another man called Richmond, who is wanted for certain hideous murders in the West of the United States, and whose uncouth appearance conceals a murderous and macabre mind; and a young lady called Helen, who in her wanton perversity rivals even myself, and with whom I had established relations of a sexually intimate nature. I persuaded her to involve me in their scheme, and after Lipsius had perused several of my literary compositions, he consented to my inclusion of what he called the Blood Quest. I therefore joined that august theatrical company of which Davies is the director, Helen the leading lady, and Richmond the stage manager, joined it, I say, in the capacity of writer. I was to be the Oscar Wilde to their Henry Beerbohm Tree, Ellen Terry, and Bram Stoker.

'I insisted that it was necessary to reflect upon the nature of the characters in this, my first experiment in drama. Especially, I required some clear information concerning the personality and habits of the Victim, who would no doubt be admirably played by Mr Charles Renshawe. Richmond therefore sought out an associate of his, and slaughtered him, but not before extracting for my delectation all the items of information which I required.

'And so I wrote my play. It was performed over the last few weeks in the streets of London, and was greeted with unprecedented applause by all who were so privileged as to see it. As I said earlier, the leading male role was played by Mr Charles Renshawe, outdoing himself in the part of an amateur detective; the female lead was played most engagingly by his intimate friend, Lady Clarissa Mountford, who imparted to the drama a dash of unexpected panache; Mr Davies was his usual polished and assured self, something he does with rare accomplishment, as Mr Harold Sedgemoor, scholar and gentleman, and as Mr Montague Raymond, connoisseur of the curious and unusual; Mr Richmond showed improvement in the role of Henry Potter, assistant at a private madhouse, and responded to the unforeseen adlibbing of Mr Renshawe with laudable vigour as Mr Herbert Tanner; Miss Helen delighted her large circle of admirers by taking on the seemingly incompatible parts of Arabella Wesley and Deborah Mornington, and acting memorably in both; I made my first stage appearance as the Young Lady with Flaming Red Hair; and three rogues briefly occupied the stage for an impeccably choreographed fight scene.

'The plot depended upon the irony of seducing the Magician, Renshawe, into a Devil's Maze, in which we prompted him to befuddle himself with his own thoughts. He thought he was "seeing through" a plot in which impostors hunted for their victim, and became convinced of his own spurious knowledge. It was really so easy to ensure that he abandoned all precautions and walked unsuspectingly into our trap. And I relied on you, Lady Clarissa, to reinforce his false picture of what was occurring and thus further snare him in a web of delusion.

'An an author, I trust I may be permitted my conceits and ornamentations. I embellished my drama by giving my confederates certain of my manuscripts. I had much pleasure in the thought that they were at last seeing publication before so select an audience. Moreover, they served to confuse the two main characters even further, and forwarded the progress of the insane suspicion that they no longer knew what was real. I find it all superlatively ironic.

'But I must confess to an egoism that impelled me to make Septimus Keen the main character, especially since he is never seen. He is only experienced by means of his art. I am thus the centre of my own mad maze.

'My tales cannot be dismissed as fantasies. They are truer than the reality which Renshawe thought he was experiencing. Each one of them is based upon my own inner life. They are confessions of my ecstasies and my pain.

'But let us return to the climax of my play. At

this point in time, Renshawe is in the engrossing company of Miss Deborah Mornington, and will soon be at her mercy. Lady Clarissa Mountford is ignorant of these developments, but is in the process of becoming enlightened. Perhaps even now, Renshawe lies prone upon the floor, the victim of a drugged glass of port, ready to be stripped, bound and delivered, signed and sealed, one might say, into the eager hands of Dr Lipsius . . .

'The ending seems a little predictable, does it not? And predictability runs contrary to the idea of style. I have some little loyalty to Lipsius, but I am owned entirely by the Goddess of Literature. I therefore sought for an inspired alternative ending, and I found one.

'I knew that after delivering Renshawe to Lipsius, Helen would take a handsom cab and collect Davies, Richmond and myself, in that order, and we would all proceed to the doctor's for an evening and night of mirth, torture, and festivity. I therefore resolved upon writing a full account of my play, and delivering it to Lady Clarissa Mountford, who would read it, and, if I gave her the address, rush to the assistance of Renshawe. At my own place of residence, I have left with my manservant a manuscript for my former confederates, which will inform them of what I have done.

'Their astonishment will be comical, but that cannot compare with the amazement which Lipsius will feel when he is caught red-handed, after which he will no doubt face the gallows. I think Comedy must be my forte; it is so much more stylish than Tragedy. It is a splendidly perverse ending, is it not?

'Note too the inspiration it gives me for a sequel. For Davies, Richmond and Helen from now on really will be hunting for a Young Lady with Flaming Red Hair. The eternal dream of the author will have occurred, for what I conceived in my imagination really will come to pass. It will be a pleasure to write a drama in which my facility for disguise enables me to outwit these actors.

'Thank you for your bemused applause, Lady Mountford. I have always admired you from afar, and dreamed of your love. I cannot evoke it, so I evoke instead your begruding admiration. Your part is written. Please do not fail me.

'The house is Number Thirteen, Sheen Street.'

*   *   *   *   *   *

Clarissa laid down the manuscript, barely able to believe what she had just read. She swallowed what remained of her brandy, and resolved upon another immediately. Of course there was no question of her not going to Sheen Street. That pompous idiot, Lord Selkirk, could do some useful work for a change.

10

The Adventure of the
Respectable Residences

Charles Renshawe lay on a stone slab. His arms and legs were chained to it. The room was fast shuttered and curtained, and its only illumination came from tall black candles. His eyes could perceive only the statue of a goat upon an altar, and seated below it, a portly man of middle age, whose head was bald at the crown, and whom he knew to be Dr Lipsius. His body smarted and ached from the light scourging it had received, and trickles of blood had dried upon his body.

'It must be awfully painful reflecting on how you came to be here, Mr Renshawe,' Dr Lipsius was saying. 'I must confess how much I enjoyed telling you about the play by Miss Veronica Parke. She will achieve much in the world of drama, I think, do you not agree, my dear sir? But then I had forgotten. You never agree with anything I say, Mr Renshawe. But allow me to give utterance to one proposition to which I shall compel your assent. I have your permission? Capital! The proposition is this: that you will suffer pain tonight Mr Renshawe, that you will travel to the utmost limits

249

of pain tonight Mr Renshawe, that you will experience pain in a manner which you never suspected possible, Mr Renshawe.' Lipsius licked his thin lips briefly.

'An interesting prospect, is it not?' he continued. 'Try as you might, you will end up begging me to stop, even though you know that I will not stop. Forgive me for wearying you with my discourse, my dear sir, but psychology has always held me in her thrall. You may think that your travels in the East have familiarised you with practices which grant immunity from pain. Pardon my laughter. I also have traveled in the East, and I have learned other practices, which concern the infliction of pain, and against the agonising embrace of which nothing is proof. Your plight almost makes me want to experience the emotion of pity, but then I never allow emotions to interfere with questions of style.'

Lipsius savoured a sip of sherry, and was about to resume his mocking monologue, when there came two respectful taps upon the door, announcing the presence of the butler.

'Ah, I do believe that my disciples desire to enter,' he remarked. 'Both Miss Mornington and Mr Sedgemoor are most eager to welcome you, I know. I gather that Sedgemoor wishes to resume your absorbing discussing of aesthetics.' Lipsius walked slowly to the door, his small, plump hands toying with the gleaming sacrificial knife.

He turned several keys, drew back the bolt, opened the door, and gaped past the terrified eyes of the butler into the muzzle of a derringer held by the gloved fingers of Clarissa Mountford. Next to her stood a gentleman with a revolver.

Dr Lipsius did not hesitate. The knife he was holding slid between his ribs and into his heart.

Approximately one hour later, Renshawe lay back in Clarissa's carriage, almost as exhausted by police questioning as by his ordeal. He left conversation to Lord Selkirk, who was holding forth on his solution to the problem of the criminal classes. Clarissa sat to Charles Renshawe, gently stroking his hand. From time to time, she glanced out of the window, as if to ensure that a drama of the damned was not once more blazing in the grimy streets of the great city. It was with a sense of relief that she sighted the rows of elegant Kensington houses. In a moment, the brougham would draw up outside the front door.

'I say, how extraordinary!' Lord Selkirk cried suddenly. 'Look out of the window a moment. There is a hackney coach outside the house if I am not mistaken, and it does not have any horses. I always thought hackney coaches were a relic of another age.'

The carriage drew up next to the abandoned hackney coach, and its three passengers descended to the pavement. Lord Selkirk was the first to look in through the window of the vehicle, and he recoiled in horror at what he saw. Renshawe and Clarissa looked, and felt the blood drain from their faces.

Lying in the coach was what had once been a human being. Its face was unrecognisable, for it had been clawed, as if by some ravenous cat, and there was blood in place of the eye-sockets. Upon the body had been etched with knives a series of whorls, symbols and designs, one of which was the reversed swastika. The limbs had been mutilated virtually beyond recognition, and were unclothed save for a few scraps of women's apparel. The hair, now thick and matted with crimson wetness, was long, and a flaming red. But lower down, beneath the complex series of red crisscrossing patterns that was the belly, was the remains of something that gave them the unmistakable information of the victim's sex. It was a man.

'Septimus Keen.' said Mr Charles Renshawe.

Epilogue

By the Author

I have always been a fervent admirer of the work of Arthur Machen, and his *The Three Impostors* has always held an especial appeal for me. Those who know and love Machen's work are unfortunately few and far between, and I rejoiced to find one day in a Kentish Town pub, an old gentleman who professed a similar admiration.

Over a series of pints which were called 'ale,' but which were not, and which did not cost fourpence, he told me that he used to know someone who knew Machin briefly when the latter was living and struggling to write in London in the eighteen nineties. This mutual acquaintance was apparently a great friend of my informant, was himself a writer, and called himself Septimus Keen.

I subsequently visited this old man in a room in Highbury, in order to learn more both of Machen and of Keen. I learned that the latter, who had sometimes affected ladies' apparel, was found murdered in a hackney coach on April 21st 1900. A yellowed clipping from the *Daily Mail* informed me that the body had been hideously mutilated. The criminals were apparently never discovered.

I asked the old man if he possessed any further information, and he answered by passing me a series of bulky files which contained both the work of Septimus Keen, and certain of his private papers. I was sufficiently excited by the discovery to contemplate a biography, and I subsequently passed many hours in studying these papers within the confines of this shabbily furnished single room.

It appears that Keen, who relates that he was born in London on October 15th 1870, knew many of the minor literary figures of the age. A diary, which he kept haphazardly, mentions a luncheon appointment with M. P. Shiel, and another entry tells of his having drunk absinthe with John Davidson. There is a copy of Aleister Crowley's *White Stains,* privately printed for presentation to friends, and signed by the author, who heads his signature: 'To Septimus—a poet like myself.' And there is a note from Arthur Machen inviting him to call upon him and sample wine from Touraine.

The literary productions are of uneven quality, consisting as they do mainly of fragments, though there is a fine short story or two. There is also a novel which is so exceedingly pornographic that it could not be published today. Most interesting of all, however, was a sketch for a novel to be entitled *The Hunted and the Hunters,* which was dated January 12th 1900.

256

The notes inform us that Arthur Machen had told Keen that after he 'entered the portals of a certain secret order', the characters in his book *The Three Impostors* actually entered his life and related extraordinary tales to him. We find confirmation of this assertion in Machen's *Autobiography* and in his *The London Adventure*. Septimus Keen's comment is: 'So he has at last realised that his dreams do exist around him . . .' This is succeeded by the following remarks:

'Machen's book cries out for a sequel from another point of view. I cannot describe as he can, nor can I evoke wonder from the commonplace, but I do not intend to. I shall give to his truth an alternative perception.'

All that remains of *The Hunted and the Hunters* are notes concerning the characters and plot, and the complete version of *The History of the Young Lady with Flaming Red Hair*. I was enchanted by the strangeness of the conception, and taking that story as my starting point, I proceeded to write what I hoped might be the novel he intended before his mysterious death.

All crudeness is due solely to my inexperienced pen. Keen admitted that he was no Machen, and I am no Septimus Keen. I can only hope that the reader will pardon my interpretation of Septimus Keen's notes. I have remained faithful to every jotting, and my own poor handiwork is especially to be discerned in the last chapter, for Keen left no indication of how his novel would be finished.

I thought it appropriate to end with the account of Keen's bizarre death: I myself remain uncertain of how much of his projected novel was fact and how much was fiction. The more deeply one studies this author, the more blurred does the distinction become. This is particularly true of his short stories, where I must acknowledge a debt both to him for the ideas, and to the American writer of weird fiction, H.P. Lovecraft, with whom the reader may detect certain affinities.

I sincerely hope that the result has at least been entertaining. For my own part, I am still at work on my biography, and would be most grateful if anyone who has the good fortune to be in possession of any scrap of information concerning Septimus Keen could contact me.

Gerald Suster

Cassie did not feel the Soul Rider enter her body . . . but suddenly she knew that Anchor was corrupt. Knew that the Flux beyond Anchor was no formless void, from which could issue only mutant changelings and evil wizards . . . Flux was the source of Anchor's existence! The price of her knowledge is exile – the first confrontation with the Seven Who Wait for the redemption of World . . .

The Weerde
Book 1
Devised by Neil Gaiman, Mary Gentle and Roz Kaveney

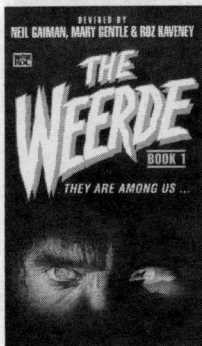

In the Library of the Conspiracy many theories are pursued in rare books and documents supplied by a caste of white-gloved librarians. Many wild-eyed researchers piece together their elaborate nonsenses of Templars, Vampires and Illuminati.

But one such theory weaves like a constant thread of darkness through human history. The rumour of an ancient race, more powerful than we are: elusive, terrifying, offering sexual frenzy but bringing madness and early death.

These are the tales of the Weerde, the shape-shifting predators of which occult legend speaks. They are plausible, charming, different and very, very dangerous.

The Weerde contains eleven chilling stories that expose the terrifying truth behind the conspiracy. Their authors are Storm Constantine, Mary Gentle, Colin Greenland, Brian Stableford, Josephine Saxton, Charles Stross, Roz Kaveney, Paul Cornell, Chris Amies, Michael Fearn and Liz Holliday.

RoC

**Exploring New Realms
in Science Fiction/Fantasy Adventure**

Villains!
Devised by Mary Gentle
and Neil Gaiman

Who needs heroes anyway?

These are the untold stories – the other side of the Legend. For in the Twenty Four Kingdoms lie those dark and dangerous places inhabited by halfling assassins, corrupt warriors and necromancers, evil princesses, and wickedly clever orcs ... the world of sword and sorcery as it really is!

At last the time has come to enter in their company the slums, mountains, cities and wilderness; to cross the boundaries of the Dark Land itself – and hear the *real* truth.

Because just for once the Dark Lords, mercenaries, money-grubbing dwarves and monsters are the stars of these new tales from Mary Gentle, Storm Constantine, Stephen Baxter, Keith Brooke, David Langford, Charles Stross, Alex Stewart, James Wallis, Roz Kaveney, Paula Wakefield, Molly Brown and Graham Higgins.

And just for once – the bad guys may even win!

RoC

**Exploring New Realms
in Science Fiction/Fantasy Adventure**

The Artificial Kid
by Bruce Sterling

**The mind-bending novel of a savage, shifting future world, by
the SF king of cyberpunk.**

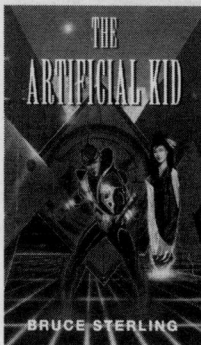

Shallow seas, coral-atoll continents, flying islands – this is the
world of Reverie, the Artificial Kid its most notorious video
star, a professional combat artist who tapes his act of violence
for sale to an avid public.

But the Kid's affluent lifestyle is less predictable than he
imagines – especially when he has to flee from the Cabal with
Moses Moses, newly emerged from seven hundred years of
suspended animation. Then the mysterious forces that come
into play have drastic effects – both on him and the lovely
Saint Anne Twiceborn.

Vampire World 1:
Blood Brothers
by Brian Lumley

In the beginning, on Starside, Harry Keogh *was* The Source. Ultimately he would also be the Doombringer – to the Old Wamphyri. But death is not the end: not for Harry, nor for the vampires whose tenacity is legendary.

The prime maxim of the Necroscope was always this: 'What will be, has been …' But who may read the future with impunity? NO man! Who is there now to talk with the Teeming Dead and recover the long-lost secrets of the tomb? With the Necroscope gone, who is left to oppose THE RETURN OF THE WAMPHYRI?

On Sunside dwells a woman with a secret. Nana Kiklu, Szgany widow, is the mother of twin sons – and their father was Harry Keogh! In their hands lies the terrifying future of the *Vampire World* – and maybe of our own planet, too…

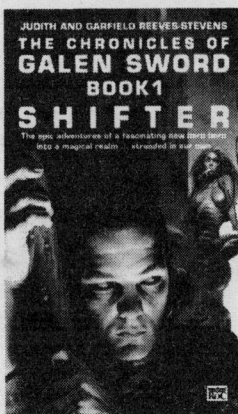